My Take Out At The Old Ball Game

To Lynn:
Hope you enjoy
the book.

Dave

To Lynn!
Hope you enjoy
the book.
Love

My Take Out At The Old Ball Game

By
Dave Hinrichs

E-BookTime, LLC
Montgomery, Alabama

My Take Out At The Old Ball Game

Library of Congress Control Number: 2012943444

ISBN: 978-1-60862-410-2

First Edition
Published July 2012
E-BookTime, LLC
6598 Pumpkin Road
Montgomery, AL 36108
www.e-booktime.com

In Memory of Lionel White

Prado

I was waiting in line at a concession stand to get a cup of beer and a hot dog when I saw Stratton Papademetriou strolling through the concourse. He was wearing a red knit shirt with a Redvale Phillies logo on it and carrying a plastic tray full of wrapped coin rolls. I stared right at him, and he walked past me without a glance and stopped at a French fry stand and gave the tray to a fat woman with a mole the size of half dollar on her cheek. She wiped the palms of her hands on her greasy apron and handed him a bank bag. Right here, I should say I thought I saw Stratton Papademetriou strolling through the concourse because first, nobody in his right mind would give Pappy a job handling money, and second, he was living with his aunt in Columbiana, Ohio the last I heard. As he walked back past me, I glimpsed the name on the I.D. tag hanging around his neck, and snapped my fingers, remembering something Pappy had told me during one of our conversations while working on the prison road crew. He stopped at a door marked:

**Private
Club Personnel Only**

He punched in a security code and went into a corridor leading to the offices behind the ticket windows.

I climbed up to the last row of seats in the general admission section of the bleachers along the first base line in time to see the eight-hole hitter for Akron hit a mile high pop-up to the infield. The last time I was in Municipal Memorial Stadium – It's named after some energy company now because the company paid the club owner a pile of money for the naming rights. The last time I was here was in 1982, and I wasn't sitting in the bleachers; I was on the mound pitching a three hitter for the Lynn Sailors.

I won fifteen games that year with a 2.87 earned run average. I was only twenty-three years old. The Sailors didn't have a parent club, and during the off-season, the club owner sold my contract to the San Diego Padres, making a nice profit for himself off my right arm. I went to spring training with the big club and then started the season with the Las Vegas Stars in the Pacific Coast League. Cashman Field was completed just in time for the season opener; they were trucking in palm and olive trees to landscape the stadium right up until game time. The ball would carry well in the desert heat, but the park had deep power alleys and the centerfield fence was over 430 feet away. I remember standing on the mound with my back to the plate in the 110 degree heat and gazing over the right field wall at the snowcapped mountains in the distance. I loved the dry heat. It was easy to get loose, and there was no humidity to sap your strength. I started the season 5-0, and I had the hitters tied up in knots. You never saw so many check swings for strikes in your life. I didn't have a great fastball, but I had movement on it. I had a cut-fastball that I ran in on the lefthanders, a two-seamer that sunk and a four-seamer I could bring up to the dish at close to ninety an hour. I had two speeds on my curve, a slider, and a helluva three-finger change-up I loved to spot, and I could throw them all for strikes. My first year in professional ball, my pitching coach in the Pioneer League told me if wanted to be successful never throw the same pitch in the same location twice in a row. I never forgot that piece of advice. Nowadays, too many pitchers just try to rear back and throw the ball past the hitters, but I don't care if you can hump it up there at 100 miles an hour, the good hitters are going to catch up with the fastball and knock the shit out if it. Even as a kid, I knew how to set up a hitter; I could move the ball around the strike zone and change speeds. I knew how to work a hitter, and I also brought a mean disposition to the mound. If anybody took me deep, he could be sure I'd put him on his back the next time he came to the plate. You had to make them pay; if they took something from you, you had to make them pay. You let these hitters keep leaning in and leaning in, and next thing you know they think they own the plate, and they're hanging over it like goddamned baboons. If a hitter leaned in on me, I moved them off the plate fast with some chin music.

I opened up with a couple of no decisions, and then I won my next five starts. I was really in a groove. Then in early June I pitched in Portland. It was a cool, damp night, and I had trouble getting loose in the bullpen. There had been a heavy rain before the game, and it started up again during the game, and the mound was in bad shape. They didn't take care of the fields in the minor leagues like they did the majors. In the bottom of the fourth inning, there was a runner on third with one out, and I had two strikes on the batter. I tried to put some extra bite on a slider, but my plant foot slipped, and I felt something pop loose in my elbow and roll right up my arm like a window shade. That was the last pitch I threw that year. I'd torn the ulnar collateral ligament in my arm, which isn't too bad unless you're a pitcher and then it's very bad. They operated on me and replaced the ligament with a tendon from my leg. My arm was in a brace for a month, and I wasn't allowed to even pick up a baseball for another five months. When I reported to spring training, I wasn't ready to pitch in any cactus league games, so when the squads broke camp they left me behind in Yuma to rehab, but I never was able to find my way back to the pitcher I was before I hurt my arm. I worked out with the Arizona Western College baseball squad for a couple of months, and spent the rest of the season in the California League except for a couple of starts with the Padres Double A team in Mobile at the end of the year, and then I pitched winter ball in Venezuela. I started the next season with Las Vegas, but any resemblance between me and the pitcher who was the ace of the staff in '83 was strictly coincidental. I could throw as hard as ever, but I'd lost the movement on my fastball and any consistency with my breaking stuff. Then I got desperate and started experimenting during games, which is the worst thing a pitcher can do, and messed up my mechanics and developed shoulder problems. I tried to pitch through the shoulder pain, but by that time I'd lost all confidence in my stuff, and when that happens to a pitcher, he's finished. He starts nibbling at the plate instead of going right after the batter and making him hit his pitch.

The last game I ever pitched in professional ball was a road game against Utah on a hot Sunday afternoon in July. We were getting hammered ten or twelve to nothing in the seventh when I came into the game. I'd been relegated to mop up duty by then. The first guy I faced was their three-hole hitter – a lanky first baseman who was black as coal with a nose spread across his face and an Afro sprouting out from under his batting helmet. The first pitch I threw was a fastball that came straight down the pike, and he turned on it and hooked a wicked foul into the seats down the right field line that nearly decapitated a fan. The next pitch I threw was a slow curve that floated up to the plate at belt level like a beach ball, and those white eyes of his looked like saucers as he waited for the ball. He must have hit it about 500 feet over the scoreboard in right center field. I was pissed off to begin with, but he watched the flight of the ball and then flicked the bat over his shoulder and gave our dugout a look before he started jogging around the bases. It seemed like a white hot switch turned on in my brain – I was so mad I couldn't see straight. I called that nigger bastard every name I could think of as he went around the bases, and when the cleanup hitter started moving the dirt around at the plate and digging in, I yelled in at him, "Keep on digging because that's right where I'm gonna bury you!" I tried to hit him in the ribs with a fastball, but it sailed and nailed him square on the ear hole. The ball bounced all the way back to the mound, and the batter went down like he was pole-axed. The benches emptied, and during the brawl, their first base coach – an old-timer – broke his collarbone. The batter ended up with a bruised jaw and a concussion. They'd been having a lot of bench clearing brawls in the league that year, so I guess the president wanted to make an example of me, and he suspended me for twenty-five games. To compound my problems, while I was suspended, I got into a fight with a guy at a bar on the Strip over some girl and ended up breaking his nose. The cops hauled me in and charged me with felonious assault, resisting arrest, disturbing the peace and every other damn charge they could come up with. When the club heard about it, they released me and invoked the clause in my contract about conduct detrimental to the team and refused to pay me. Now, if I would've been pitching good, I could've kicked the dog and beat the wife and the club would've looked the other way, but when your earned run average is over five, they show you the door. On the Strip, they call it the fast shuffle.

I wound up doing a six-month stretch in the Southern Desert Correctional Facility. That was my first stretch in the can, and it was quite a come down from people asking for my autograph and waiting outside the clubhouse door for me after games and getting comped all over town because I was a ballplayer. I was just another number in jail. While I was inside, I fell in with a gambler by the name of Ely Lovelock who was in the can for not paying his child support. He was a big baseball fan and had seen me pitch a couple of times. So to pass the time when we weren't pressing license plates or sweeping up sawdust in the wood shop, I told him stories about life in the minors and he told me stories about all the money he'd won and lost gambling. He had gone through a lot of wives and a lot of money. When he got out, he asked me to look him up in Boulder City after I was released because he might have a job for me – what kind of job, he wouldn't say.

I brushed it off figuring I'd latch on with another organization after I got out. I didn't know then I'd burned all my bridges back into baseball. The season had started when I was released, and no organization wanted to take the risk of plopping a guy fresh from jail onto one of their rosters. Nobody would take a chance on me except a couple of teams in one of the independent leagues, but they paid next to nothing, so I hung around Vegas for awhile – my apartment was leased to the end of the year. I applied for unemployment benefits, but all I got was a letter stating that "Determination of ineligibility for compensation is based on reason for termination ("see sub-section c) from most recent employer." I waited until I was down to my last dollar, and then I took a bus over to Boulder City.

You've heard about what happens when you get on that slippery slope; well, I was on it, and it took me straight down to Ely Lovelock's doorstep. He'd cooked up a plan to rip off the casinos by using an electric wheelchair, an electromagnet and a pair of loaded dice at the craps tables. Three people were needed

11

to execute the scam: a shooter – him, a guy in a wheelchair – his paraplegic cousin, and a blocker – that was the job Lovelock had in mind for me if I decided to come in on it. I was going to be a late bettor who blocks the view of the stickman. Lovelock had set up a makeshift craps table in his dining room complete with a twelve foot felt craps layout, chips, casino dice, a rattan dice stick – everything he'd need to rehearse the scam until he had it down to a science. It required perfect timing – perfect coordination between the three of us – I was in, by the way. Lovelock fast-talked me into it with a pitch about how we'd make the rounds of all the casinos and not make more than one or two passes with the dice at each casino, and if for some reason any of us didn't like the layout at a casino, we'd split and be out the door to the next place. We wouldn't push it, wouldn't get greedy – We'd low key it and not overwork the grift. I was figuring along the lines of my share giving me some breathing room and letting me concentrate on hooking up with another organization.

I had to admit, it was an ingenious grift, but it would have to be choreographed perfectly for it to work because there was going to be a lot of eyes on us – the boxman, the croupier, the floating security staff, the robotic eye-in-the-sky video surveillance. The bilk job all started with Lovelock palming a pair of loaded dice and switching them with the house dice – I'll tell you, he was a regular Houdini with the slight of hand. I'd stand two feet away from him watching his every move, and I wasn't able to tell how he switched the dice. His cousin, a bloated, bald-headed object of sympathy in his wheelchair, would be situated at the other end next to the angled-rubber wall guard on the back wall of the table, and I'd be positioned between him and the croupier. When Lovelock would throw the dice, I'd lean in to place a late bet, blocking the croupier's view of him. Placing a bet after the dice are rolled isn't illegal as long as the dice are still rolling, but the way we were going to play it was illegal because we knew how those dice were going to come up. At the same time I was leaning in, I'd say something stupid like, "There goes the money for the girlfriend's abortion," and look the boxman right in the eye to distract him. Lovelock's cousin would lean forward to get a better view of the table, and as soon as the dice bounced back off the rubber, he'd touch a button on the side of the wheelchair hidden by his jacket to turn on the electromagnet powered by the electric battery of the wheelchair and those dice would come up seven – a winner!

We practiced and practiced until we could do it in our sleep, but doing it in Lovelock's apartment was different than doing it in a casino where one little slip up meant a long mandatory jail sentence. When we finally agreed we were ready, we hit a small casino first – The Desert Star – a block off the Strip. The first time I walked up to the craps table, I was in a cold sweat and my knees were shaking – I was nervous as hell. I felt like there were a million eyes on me, but it went off smoothly, almost too smoothly. We were supposed to be complete strangers to each other, so we didn't come in contact until the next craps table at the next casino. We hit three other casinos that day which I thought was pushing our luck, but we pulled it off, and by the end of the day we'd raked in close to ten grand.

Lovelock wanted to hit a few more places in Vegas right away and then expand the grift up to Carson City and Reno, but I was developing a severe case of cold feet. I finally convinced him to lay low for a little while. He was like every other degenerate gambler I've ever known. He just couldn't leave well enough alone and quit while he was ahead. He had to milk it for all it was worth until it ran dry, and then it was too late to let go. In the end, they were all looking to lose – one way or another.

Lovelock was amazing to watch at the table because there was nothing to see. He was slick as hell the way he switched the loaded dice with the house dice and back again, but it reminded me of what happens when you tip your pitches. You can bring great stuff to the table, but if a guy knows what to look for, you're going to get creamed. It's not a matter of balls or brains because getting paid isn't the hard part, it's keeping the suspicion off you. Once they get wind of you, they just curl up in the shadows and focus all that technology and attention on you and toy with you until they're good and ready to pounce, and when they come down on you, it's like the Sword of God.

I knew I shouldn't have gone in with Lovelock in the first place, and I sure as hell knew I should've cut and run with my share of the scam – get while the getting was good and try to pick up the pieces of my baseball career, but I didn't, and I still can't figure out why. Maybe it was because deep down I knew my arm was shot at twenty-five, and there wasn't going to be any career in the big leagues, and I was going to wind up like every other slob slogging through the miserable routine of life, collecting a crummy paycheck – run of the mill mediocrities and dullards – rabble just happy for a hot dog and a hump. Maybe I was just pissed off I'd been screwed over in my life, and it was time to make somebody start paying for it. Of course, I was too young then to realize I was going to be paying for a long time.

Our luck came to an end at a place on the strip called the Oasis. I still don't know what tipped them off to us; they never told us. Maybe Lovelock was like that pitcher tipping his pitches, and somebody read his delivery because he made one pass and was about to throw the dice again when a security guy grabbed him around the neck and got him in an arm lock and kept applying the pressure until his hand opened and those palmed dice fell out on the floor. Another security guard grabbed him by the other arm, and they dragged him away. I started to casually back away from the craps table, but an army of security guards put a stop to that by tackling me. They didn't have to worry about old baldy making a break for it. They rolled him into a backroom with the rest of us.

In Vegas, they call it being back-roomed, and it's about as pleasant as having your wisdom teeth pulled without Novocain. The powers that be forcefully impress upon you how bad it is to try to cheat the casino and how bad it would be to ever – ever enter the casino again. They impress this upon you by hurting you anyway they please, and you're almost grateful for this because their other option is to send you to jail for a long time. Some casinos – like the Oasis – don't want the publicity of a trial because the testimony gives other scam artists ideas, so they just hurt you the first time.

The backroom they took us into had a long wooden table in the middle of it. The only light was coming from a bare bulb hanging over the table. There were several folding chairs along one wall and stacks of plastic dairy and soda crates against the other walls. A half dozen security guards sat Lovelock and me down while another one wheeled his cousin over to the table. The guards hovering over us were dressed in gray slacks and blue blazers with silver name tags. Their boss looked like he'd been poured into his clothing by a cement mixer. He was bulging at the seams of his jacket, and it was all muscle. His arms hung down from his broad shoulders like a monkey's. He had a round face with blubbery lips, a flat nose, beady eyes, and a sparse flat top as black and bristly as the hair on a pig's back. He was wearing horn-rimmed glasses that didn't go with his course features. He went over to the table and sat on it, swinging his squat legs. No one said a word; they seemed to be waiting for somebody. Then the door opened and a tall, blond-haired guy in an expensive suit and French cuffs came in. According to his name tag, he was the operations chief. He whispered to the guy sitting on the table for a minute and then left. As soon as the door closed, the muscle-bound guy hopped off the table and nodded at the guards standing over Lovelock, and without a word, they picked him up by the arms and legs, carried him over to the table and dropped him flat on his back. His face was white as chalk under the bare bulb, and his terror-stricken eyes were darting back and forth in his head trying to read something in the faces of the guards holding him down. Their boss was standing with his back to Lovelock's cousin, and I noticed he was holding a ball-peen hammer at his side. Lovelock couldn't see it because it was below the table level.

"Did you ever wonder what it's like to be stuck in a wheelchair?" he asked Lovelock, and I knew what he was going to do to him, but I didn't look away because if Lovelock had to take it, I could at least have the guts to watch it.

"Ple-e-e-ase," Lovelock squeaked.

"I said did you ever wonder what it's like to be stuck in a wheelchair?" the guard's tone had turned hard.

"No...Ye-s-s-s, I guess...yes."

He swung the hammer in a quick arc and hit Lovelock on the right kneecap, and before Lovelock could even scream, he'd hit him again on the left kneecap, cracking both of them like walnut shells. Lovelock screeched so loud the players out on the casino floor must have heard him unless the room was soundproof. The guards let go of him, and he curled up in a fetal position, squirming and screaming in agony, holding his knees.

"Now you won't have to wonder anymore," the guard said over his screams. He dropped the hammer on the floor and walked over to me, and when I saw the little smirk on his face, I stood up and two guards grabbed me around the arms and tried to sit me down. Lovelock's cousin was bawling in the background, his hands covering his face, managing to whimper, "Don't hurt me," between sobs.

"Going somewhere?" the guard snarled at me. "We're not done here, so sit down asshole." The smirk had returned, and all I wanted to do was wipe it off his fat, ugly face, so I pushed back on the guards, using them for leverage, and swung my leg up and kicked him right in the belly. His glasses flew off, and he went down on his knees with a loud gasp and stayed there, wheezing, trying to get some air back into his lungs. Meanwhile, a few more guards jumped on me, knocking me to the cement floor. Their boss got to his feet with some help, picked up his glasses, and checked them for scratches. "Get him up!" he ordered the guards piled on top of me. They pulled me to my feet while he breathed on his glasses and wiped them with a handkerchief. "Hold him up...get his legs."

When they were holding me tight as a vice, and I couldn't move a muscle, he stood nose to nose with me. "A real hard ass, huh?" he spit at me.

"Fuck you!" I spit back. "Fuck all you bastards."

He took a step back and punched me in the nose, and I tasted the blood in the back of my throat as gobs of it poured out of my broken nose over the front of my shirt. Then he really loaded up and nailed me on the cheekbone with a right hand. My head snapped back and the room started to tilt, but before I blacked out I felt one last hook in the ribs.

When I woke up, I was lying in the back of the cousin's handicap-equipped van next to Lovelock who was groaning slow and steady. I heard the van engine turn over and someone's voice on the driver's side saying, "...Just follow Interstate Fifteen right out of town and keep going...and don't ever come back." Then the door slammed shut and the van started moving.

I never saw Lovelock or his cousin again after that night. They never went back to Vegas, but I did. I licked my wounds and bided my time, and three months later I was back in Vegas staking out the Oasis to find out that bastard's work schedule – where he lived and how he got to and from work. I found out he had an apartment about a mile from the casino, got off work at 8:00 p.m. or 4:00 a.m. depending on his shift and usually walked to work for the exercise.

One night, I let the air out of a tire of a car parked on a dark section of Durango Drive, pried off the hub cap with a tire iron, and waited for him to come walking by on his way home from the casino. When he came by, I pulled my baseball cap over my eyes, hunched down over the flat tire, and asked him if he could give me a hand. He stopped and muttered something, and when he came over to the curb, I spun around and clipped him on the head to calm his nerves. Then I took that tire iron and stuck it about three inches into his eye socket and twisted it around in there a couple of times to see what I could dredge up. I took off running and left Vegas that night and haven't been back since. Much later, I heard he was still working at the Oasis – not on the security staff, of course, because he had a glass eye and his left arm was paralyzed from brain damage. You had to make them pay.

I managed to latch on with a team in the Arizona Fall League in '86, but I couldn't throw worth a shit anymore because of the pain in my shoulder. The doctor did tests – x-rays and special imaging – and found a partial rotator cuff tear and recommended rest, anti-inflammatory medication and more rehab.

I worked out for a few teams in spring training the following year, but I was still having pain, and this time the doctor said I needed open reconstruction of the shoulder, and my career was probably over. There was no probably about it; my career – such as it was – was over at twenty-eight. I tried to find another job in baseball – I would've taken practically anything – but had no luck. Then I tried to get a coaching job at the college level, but I never could get past the criminal background check. Some things you keep paying for over and over.

I went back east to New Jersey where I was born and ended up getting a bartending job in Vineland at one of those big sports bars with giant TV screens. Sometimes on my day off, I'd take a bus down to Atlantic City to play the slots or a little blackjack, but I'd steer clear of the craps tables. Once in a while, I'd do some capping or pinching to give myself an edge. If I had a good hand I'd slip an extra chip underneath my chip stack when I'd tuck my cards in and stand pat; if I had a bad hand, I'd tuck in my hand with two or three chips below the cards like I was intending to stand, and then I'd decide to take another look and scoop the chips under the cards out into my chip stack before tucking my cards back. I was just trying to reduce the house advantage a little bit. I hardly considered it cheating, but the casino did when they caught me. They didn't backroom me this time. They prosecuted me to the full extent of the law which, under the Casino Control Division of the State Attorney General's Office is very full, indeed. I got five to ten years at Riverfront State Prison; I've known murderers who got lighter sentences. That was my first long stretch, and I did five years, two months and nine days of it.

Anyway, the last time I was in Municipal Stadium – or whatever it's called now – was over sixteen years ago. I often think about where I'd be today if not for that goddamned ulnar collateral ligament. I might be sitting pretty after a successful career in the big leagues; I might have a few multi-million dollar contracts under my belt by now. Instead, I have a few stretches in prison under my belt, a 1988 Chrysler LeBaron, a suitcase and $775 dollars in my pocket – That's it. It's hard not to think about what could've been, and it's even harder not to have anyone to blame for what happened. You can't take your anger out on a piece of tendon, so you vent your anger on other targets for different reasons, and it's gotten me thrown in the can more than once. Outwardly, I don't look much different than I did sixteen years ago. I'm six foot two, still 195 pounds – no gray in the hair. I've picked up a few age lines along the way and a couple of scars, but on the outside I look pretty much the same. It's on the inside of me where it's all different. Each time you go in for a stretch something inside of you gets stripped away and you have to develop a callus over those raw spots to survive. Before you know it, the calluses harden and calcify, and instead of feelings all that's left is a hardness inside of you, and people who run up against that hard disposition could be running head first into a wall of granite for all you care about them because you're way past giving a damn about consequences.

*****

The pop up settled in the glove of the second baseman for the final out of the inning, and as the Phillies came off the field, a blaring rock song came on the public address system, cut off by the PA announcer's voice reading the seat ticket number of the lucky winner of a DVD player, followed by a run the bases for cash contest between three other lucky fans selected from the crowd. Meanwhile there must have been a half dozen mascots jumping on the dugout roofs and barging through the crowd in their furry outfits. At some point in the middle of all this bullshit, I came up with the idea to rob the ballpark. I'd been hopscotching across the state sticking up gas stations and convenience stores for nickels and dimes so I could get to the next town, and I figured, with my record, if I'm looking at twenty years in the can for stealing fifty bucks, I might as well steal two hundred grand. It had to be an inside job; there was no other way plan it. But how do you pull off an inside job if you have no one working on the inside? That was the idea I came up with.

From The Circus To A
Cabin In The Woods

The next day, I went out to the ballpark when they opened the gates at six, and I watched the boys take some batting practice. Afterwards, I took a walk around the park to check out the exits. There was a double chain link gate in the right field corner and another one next to the Phillies clubhouse in the concourse. On one side of the ticket windows was a glass double door for employees and the visitors to the club offices; on the other side were the four turnstiles and a walkway for people leaving the park. At the other end of the concourse on the third base side was a metal double door between a supply room and the visitor's clubhouse and another double chain link gate at the end of the concourse. In the left field wall, behind a picnic area, was one more chain link gate. All the gates were locked from the inside by padlocks or door locks.

When the game started, I watched a couple of innings and then went down into the concourse and hung around the concession stands across from the door to the cash room trying to get a look at what was on the other side of the door. A few people went in and out, and I managed to get a look inside at a short cement corridor leading to another door with a rectangular slot in it to slip cash drawers and bank bags through and a window the size of a porthole at eye level. I knew you might be able to get through the first door, but you weren't getting through the second door unless somebody from the other side let you in – somebody on the inside.

I went back to my seat and watched the game until the top of the seventh inning when the Phillies' pitcher tried to waste an 0-2 fastball with runners on the corners and put it in the Akron batter's wheelhouse, and he hit it into the pool behind the right field fence. That's right – a pool. The place was more like an amusement park than a ballpark. There was a pool and picnic pavilion in right field, and behind the grandstand was a putting green, a speed pitch booth, one of those inflatable things the little kids can jump around in, and a café and food court tucked under the seats. Beyond the left field fence was a deck bar that ran from the corner all the way to left-center. Behind the stands was another putting green and picnic area and arcade games. There were more brats and their moms milling around behind the grandstands than there were people sitting in the stands watching the game, and if the club wasn't spinning some promotion, it was making fans jump through hoops between innings to win some crazy contest. It was a regular goddamned circus.

I had to give credit to the owner, whoever he was; he knew how to bring people through the gates, even if it wasn't to watch the game. All that was left from when I pitched here was the original seating bowl and dugouts. There were a lot more of what you'd call revenue sources now, and all of it was funneled through the cash office into the pockets of ownership. He had a helluva deal with the city. He got all the money from the ticket sales, concessions, promotions, parking, and the city was responsible for the daily upkeep of the park. All he had to pay were the city taxes, and his payroll was small – most of the employees were seasonal, and the parent club paid the ballplayers, so he could afford to kick in some money for my favorite charity – me.

By the top of the eighth, the ticket takers were long gone, and they'd opened up all the exits, except the gates in the left and right field corners, for people who wanted to leave the game early. They didn't care if people came in off the streets. The Redvale players, to get to their clubhouse from the field, had to enter the right field side of the concourse, and when I was headed for the cafe, after checking out the lock on the mechanical room and a supply room across from the offices, I ran into the pitcher who'd given up the homer. He was taller than me – a red-faced kid with skinny forearms and big hands.

"Home run on an 0-2 count," I said as he clacked across the cement in his spikes, "cardinal sin, boy." He stopped in his tracks and turned to say something to me, but when he saw my face, he thought better of it and went in the clubhouse door.

I hadn't seen one cop in the ballpark – anywhere. I'd wandered outside and hadn't seen any cops or patrol cars there, either. I'd seen plenty of employees holding walkie-talkies and wearing Redvale Phillies caps and yellow shirts with Ballpark Ambassadors on the back, but no cops.

I bought a beer and a cheese steak, relaxed at a cafe table and waited for the game to end. People were lined up at the bar watching the game on closed circuit TV. You put down good money to buy a ticket to see a baseball game in person, and you wind up watching the game on television at a bar, anyway. That's the definition of a stupid sonofabitch.

It was hard to figure what the take would be on a job like this, not knowing how much cash the club kept on hand. I imagined they probably kept some amount of cash reserve in a safe in the cash room. Then, too, it was hard to estimate the money from the walk up tickets sales, but I calculated, between the ticket sales, advanced sales, concessions, parking and cash on hand, the take had to be in the neighborhood of two hundred grand.

I finished and threw the plastic beer cup and plate into a wire wastebasket. As I started up the ramp to the grandstand, the crowd noise rose and then fell to a disappointed moan, and I knew the Phillies had lost because the people started to pour down the ramp. I turned and went with the flow until it merged with the other flow of people from the left field grandstands, and then I dropped out and sat on a bench next to the Official Redvale Phillies Souvenir Stand.

From where I sat, I watched the concession operators at the stands counting their money and closing out their registers, but I didn't see anybody coming in or out of the cash room door. Twenty minutes later, the park had emptied out, and there was no one in the concourse except a couple of maintenance men, a club official in a red shirt and a bunch of those guys in yellow shirts.

One of them scampered over to where I was sitting and said, "Can I help you sir?"

"No."

"Are you waiting for someone?"

"No, I'm not waiting for anybody. I was just resting my legs." I straightened my legs and rubbed them.

"Do you need any assistance?" he asked. His walkie-talkie squawked on his belt.

"No, I don't need any assistance; I'll be all right, but thanks anyway."

"Well, you'll have to leave sir." His walkie-talkie squawked again, and he slipped it out of the belt holder. "We'll be closing the gates soon."

"Ohhh, I didn't realize," I stood up and stretched, and he walked away talking into the walkie-talkie. I went down the walkway past the turnstiles and another guy in a yellow shirt said good night to me and I said, "Good night, Mr. Ambassador." I'd found out what I wanted to find out; I was going into the cash room after the gates closed – not before, and I'd have to get myself a white baker's apron and one of those paper overseas caps and a red Phillies shirt at the Official Redvale Phillies Souvenir Stand.

My car was on a grass lot used for overflow parking beyond the left field wall. I drove into the big municipal lot on the other side of North Front shared by the Phillies and Carson Technology Company. Their plant and offices extended almost two blocks across from the ballpark behind a fence topped with barbed wire. I parked in the south end of the lot where I could keep an eye on the employee exit, settled down in the car seat and lit a cigarette. In the rear view mirror, I saw a water tower shaped like a giant silver lollipop rising above the long, white windowless Carson plant. I smoked the cigarette and listened to the car radio.

During the first hour, a steady stream of employees left the park for their cars in the employee lot, fewer in the next hour and fewer still in the third hour, but no Papademetriou. I'd gone through half a pack of cigarettes and was ready to leave, thinking I'd missed him or he wasn't working tonight, when I saw him come out with four other guys. They were walking in a group talking until they reached the lot and separated for their cars. Papademetriou got into a white sedan, and I started my car but left the lights off. He pulled onto Front, and I hit the lights and gave him some room.

I could've saved some time if his number would've been in the book, but it was unlisted, and the operator wouldn't give me his address, so I had to piss away three hours waiting to tail him. He made a left, and I followed him past a bunch of businesses and storefronts and a huge paint factory for three blocks to a four-lane avenue. He hung another left, drove one block and turned right between a donut shop and the high school baseball field. It was an odd street. It started out as Richland Street, and after it went under a stone railroad underpass, it changed to Hester's Lane and after another block it changed for good to Rockford Street. Papademetriou took me up past the numbered cross streets to Thirteenth. After making a right, he turned left through what looked like a college campus – athletic fields, dormitories, a tennis court. He pulled into the driveway of a brick Cape Cod on the corner of Fourteenth Street and College Avenue. I kept going straight, pulled over to the curb halfway up the block, and killed the lights. He paused on the front steps looking for his house key, and I saw his mop of curly black hair glistening under the porch light. The door swung open, and a woman's figure was silhouetted in the doorway. When he went inside, I drove to the end of the block and made a u-turn and coasted past the house. There was a wooden plaque on the wall above the mailbox with "The Papa-demetrious" burned into it. It was a long plaque. I didn't see any toys lying around on the porch or in the yard – no swing set or kiddy pool – so maybe they didn't have any kids which would sure make things a lot simpler for me.

There was very little traffic on the streets so late at night, and it only took me ten minutes to drive back through the city. I went over the Penn Street Bridge into West Redvale and after going under a railroad trestle made the first left off Penn Avenue up a steep hill to the River View Motel where I was staying. It was a stinking dump. The owner – some dago who'd lived in the country thirty years and talked like he'd just come off the boat – didn't even have set room rates. He'd dicker with you and basically settle for what you were willing to pay based on how long you intended to stay. The front desk was located in the oddest looking structure I'd ever seen: a blue corrugated, triangular building rising to a point about sixty feet high with a six foot silver tetrahedron balanced on top of it. It sat alone on top of the hill in the middle of a chewed up macadam lot. A roofed wooden walkway led down to two motel units at the bottom of the hill and a road ran around behind the units connecting the upper parking lot with the lower lot. The two units were each two stories high with alternating blue, orange and green doors. Guests staying in the second floor rooms to the rear had a view of the courthouse, some high rise apartment buildings, and part of the city set in concrete and asphalt rows at the base of the mountain on the other side of the Schuylkill River. All I saw from my window were sumac trees growing wild on the fringe of the parking lot and the blackened brick face of an abandoned factory. I don't know whose bright idea it was to name the motel River View because no one in any room had a view of the river. In the front corner on the first floor of the second unit was a cocktail lounge, closed up now following complaints by the neighbors about fights, drug dealing and prostitution in and around the lounge – all of which the owner of the motel claimed to know nothing about.

I needed some ice for the pint of scotch I had back in my room, so I stopped under the aluminum portico and went into the front desk. I kept tapping the bell until the door behind the desk opened and Cocuzza, the owner, stepped out wearing a ragged terry cloth robe – what hair he had left frizzed up behind his ears.

"Whaa you-u-u want?" he said, looking bleary-eyed at me and then the clock on the wall. It was 1:20.

"I need some ice, Mr. Cocuzza."

"Whaaa?"

"Ice," I smiled. "How you say in Italian?"

"Ahh, glacclo – non c'e giaccio. Too late...eezzz rule – no ice after midnight."

"Rule...what the hell are you talking about? You're standing right there – Get me some ice."

"I sorry...too late."

"I lost track of how late it was....Just get me some ice, all right? It'll only take you a second."

"Non...too late," he pointed at the clock, shaking his head.

"But it's never too late to be running whores up to the guests' rooms, is it?"

"Tu sei un buggiardo! Vai via! You go now."

I grabbed him by the lapels of his robe and pulled him against the counter. "Listen, you old bastard...get your ass in there and bring me some ice."

"Tu sei uno sporcaccione a parlare cosi di me."

"Say it in English," I raised my hand to slap him, and he threw his hands up to protect his face.

"You no touch me – Tu sei pazzo. Io chiamo la poliza. I call poliza."

"I let him go, and he backed out of my reach. I couldn't afford any trouble with any poliza – especially now. It'd screw up everything – all my plans. I couldn't be butting heads with any cops. "All right, take it easy...go on back to bed...you miserable old –"

"You get out...I give you trouble...all trouble you want."

"Just relax...I'm going, I'm going – no need to call the cops."

I turned to leave and heard him shout, "fuori" before the door to his living quarters slammed shut. I heard him talking in Italian to himself on the other side of the door. I guess I'd have to drink my scotch with just water.

My room had the barest of essentials: a bureau with a thousand cigarette burns in it, a metal frame bed, a chair with worn, coffee-stained upholstery which matched the threadbare carpeting, and a TV on a rusted wire stand. I turned on the air conditioner, listened to it rev up, sputter and gasp, and then rev up again before settling into a heavy *burrrrrr* that rattled the windowpane. I filled a glass halfway with scotch, put some water from the bathroom tap in it, and plopped on the bed. The room was dark except for little fingers of light on the opposite wall made by the light from the parking lot bleeding through the cracks in the drawn window shade. I took a sip of the scotch and water and gave some thought to where Pappy and the wife could hole up. The more secluded the place, the better – someplace like a cabin in the woods. I finished the drink in one gulp, took a few swigs straight from the bottle, and then rolled on my side and slept on it.

*****

The next morning I called the Redvale Phillies office and inquired if they'd had any rainouts that would be made up as a double-header, and the guy on the other end told me the league had ordered a rainout with Altoona to be made up as a twilight double-header on Saturday, August 27th, which I was very happy to hear. He went on to tell me I could purchase tickets in advance for the twilighter, but I had no intention of doing that because six bucks was six bucks. I might as well buy tickets at the walk-up window the day of the double-header and steal it back later.

I looked through the phone book but couldn't find anything under cabins and none of what was listed under campgrounds would serve the purpose. Then I got the idea to look in the Blue Pages under State Government and found Pierre Creek State Park. I called the 800 number and asked the woman who answered about cabins for rent.

"We have rustic and modern cabins for rent, sir," she said. "Rustic cabins don't have indoor plumbing –"

"I want a modern cabin," I stopped her right there.

"The modern cabins have the comforts of home – carpeting, electric heat, bedrooms, living room, kitchen and bathroom –"

"I want to rent one of those."

"They come in one or two bedrooms."

"I'd like a two bedroom cabin – the most secluded one you have. My wife and I want privacy."

"They all offer privacy, sir," she said helpfully. "But looking at the map, there is a two bedroom farther from the lake – a bit more secluded."

"That sounds fine," I said. "Now how do I go about making a reservation? I'm interested in August 25th through the 27th."

"Let me check to see if the cabin is available on those dates. Please hold a moment, sir." I heard her paging through something.

"Yes, I can make a reservation right now for you, sir. How do you wish to pay – credit card, check or money order?"

"Money order."

"Full payment is required before the 25th. The cost for a two bedroom modern is $206.97 and with the tax the total would be $223.53. The money order should be made out to Commonwealth of Pennsylvania."

"I'll get it right off to you."

"Keep in mind, the cabins are furnished and have kitchenware, but you have to bring your own bed linens, towels, toiletries...."

"Thank you, I understand –"

"If you arrive between twelve and five on the 25th," she went on, "you can pick up the key in the park office. After five, the key will be put on the ledge above the door. One more thing, sir, pets and alcohol are not permitted on the grounds."

The latter would be a tough one for Pappy, I thought.

"Would you like us to mail you a confirmation, sir?"

"No, no," I said quickly. "I don't need a confirmation – not necessary."

"Very well. All I need then is your name, address and zip code."

"My address is 1401 14th Street Redvale, and the zip code is 19605." And then I tried to say the name easily like I'd said it a million times before. "The name is Papademetriou – Mr. and Mrs. Spyridon Papademetriou."

*****

In the afternoon, I got on 724 East to a town called Grigsboro and then had to take a lot of back roads until I came to the north entrance to the park. I followed the wooden arrows nailed on the trees to the south end of Smith's Run Lake where there were two log cabins about one hundred yards apart. The one I'd reserved was the one farther down the road from the lake shore. The cabin was set on a grassy knob of land in a clearing surrounded by tall pine trees with trunks as straight as arrows. It was an A-frame with a wraparound porch and a stone grill for cookouts. There was no car in the gravel driveway, so I pulled in and looked through the crack in the curtains on the front window. I saw the Formica counter-top in the kitchen and a pine table for six. Everything was pine inside – the paneled walls, the sofa and chairs, the lamp tables. I saw the two closed doors to the bedrooms. I went around to the back of the cabin but the curtains on the bedroom windows were closed. It didn't matter; I'd seen all I needed to see. The cabin could only be seen from the short stretch of road directly in front of the place. It was a very secluded setup; it was perfect. Now all I needed was Pappy. I'd drive out to Columbiana, track him down, and bring him back with me. He might not want to come back with me, but he was coming because without him the whole plan fell apart. He was coming if I had to fold him into a neat little package and put him in the trunk, but I wouldn't have to do that. Pappy knew as well as anyone, if I came looking for a yes, God help you if you gave me a no.

The Black Greek Of The Family

Pappy and his brother immigrated from Greece to America when they were two or three years old with their parents. They lived in New York City for a few years and then moved down to Pennsylvania when Pappy's father got a job with a big kitchen company in Scranton. He was an expert cabinetmaker – a lot of those Greeks are good at working with wood. They were all living happily ever after in Scranton until the old man who apparently liked to take a drink once in a while – Hell, from what Pappy had told me, he liked to take a drink so much he'd break your arm to get the bottle from you. One night, the old man got behind the wheel with a snoot full of ouzo and pancaked the car into a bridge abutment. Not only did he kill himself, but he took the wife with him, too.

All of a sudden, the happy story in Scranton came to an end, and Pappy and his brother were orphans at sixteen. They were shipped back to New York City to live with an uncle. The uncle had a daughter, and you know where this is going before we get there, but I'll go there anyway. One day the uncle came home and caught Pappy doing something to the daughter that Greeks like to do. He beat the shit out of Pappy and had him thrown in a juvenile detention center in upstate New York where he was learning to be an auto mechanic until he stole a car he was working on, took it for a joyride, jumped the curb making a turn on a rain-slicked street, and bounced a fat woman off the side of a building like a rubber ball. The woman escaped with two broken legs, but Pappy got a transfer to a more secure place when he turned eighteen – the Oneida Correctional Facility.

While Pappy was getting an education behind bars, his brother went to college and earned some kind of degree in business. After college he moved to Philadelphia and went to work for an accounting firm. Meanwhile, Pappy moved around a lot and was never at one address for long except if it was the address of a prison. You could say the brothers had started to drift apart by this time. The Papademetrious were very clannish – the Greeks are like the dagos in that way – and Pappy had earned a reputation as the black sheep of the family. The last time Pappy saw his brother was when he visited Pappy in prison. Eventually, they lost track of each other; it's been close to ten years since they've even spoken.

The reason I know all this about Pappy is we used to talk while we were busting our backs on the road crew at Marion, or rather, he'd talk, and I'd listen. He told me a lot more about himself I can't remember or never listened to in the first place because I'd get sick of the sound of his voice. That was one of his problems – his big mouth. He never knew when to shut up; he'd keep talking and talking until he managed to talk himself right into trouble. His other problem was women.

Pappy was what you'd call a career criminal who'd never really put his heart into his work. He had a long record, but short stretches mostly on misdemeanor convictions – simple assault, disorderly conduct, disturbing the peace, petty theft, shoplifting, criminal trespass…. The fights and general carrying on were usually because of his big mouth pissing off somebody, while a woman was usually the reason behind the stealing. The four months he did in Marion was on a shoplifting charge. A girlfriend spotted a pricey pair of shoes she just had to have in the window of a mall store. He didn't have the two hundred dollars on him, so he went back to the shoe store later and had the clerk show him a pair in his girlfriend's size. Then he asked to see the same style in another color, and when the clerk went into the stockroom, he ducked out of the store with the first pair under his arm, but parking lot security collared him before he ever made it to his car.

I also knew he was inclined to take a drink once in a while; he was like his father in that regard. Normally, I'd never consider bringing a guy of his character in on a job, but I had no choice with this deal. He was the only man for this job. I'd just have to keep him in line one way or another because I saw some major pitfalls with him – the wife and him alone in a cabin for one.

*****

It's a seven hour drive from Redvale, but the timing belt broke on the Lebaron ten miles outside of Columbiana, and I had to pay for a tow to a turnpike service station, a motel room for the night and a new timing belt. When I finally got to Columbiana the next afternoon, I had $250 bucks left, and no time to waste. The first thing I did was contact the Ohio Prison Society. I remember Pappy had taken some workshops through them preparing him for his so called re-entry into society and had gotten some job referrals when he was released. I told the receptionist I was Pappy's brother and she put me through to a Mrs. Finkbinder, the director of the Society's re-entry services program. She couldn't tell me where he lived, but did tell me where he was working according to their records – Landstar Motor Express in Youngstown. When I called the trucking company, I told them I was Mr. Wilson from the Ohio Department of Rehabilitation and Correction – Parolee Records Division – and inquired as to whether Stratton Papademetriou was still an employee of the company and his current home address. They couldn't have been more helpful, and when I hung up, I hopped into my car and headed for 221 Sycamore Road.

It was eight thirty when I parked the car in front of the house at 221 Sycamore. It was a large frame home in dilapidated condition with peeling paint and missing shingles. It looked like it was being eaten away down to its shell. The third floor attic windows had been replaced by plywood, and bricks from the crumbling chimney were scattered on the porch roof. One corner of the porch was propped up by two-by-fours. There once had been a garden bordering the house but the weeds that reached almost to the windowsills had swallowed it up. The gate to the fence fronting the house was off its hinges and lying on the grass. I had no idea what hours Pappy worked, but there were lights on in the house, so I went up the walk. The casing to the doorbell was gone and the rusty button was hanging from a frayed wire. I opened the squeaky screen door and knocked on the leaded glass door. When nobody came, I banged harder and a shadow fell across the grimy rose-colored glass. A lock turned, the door opened a crack and then all the way, and Pappy was standing there in his bare feet, boxers and an undershirt.

"Pappy," I greeted him.

"Prado," he said. He managed to put a smile on his face, but he couldn't keep the fear from flooding into his eyes because he knew damn well I wasn't there on a social call.

Walking Or Sliding

He showed me into a musty smelling front parlor and sat down in an armchair with fancy carvings on the head rest. I sat myself down on the Victorian love seat. The room must've been beautiful fifty years ago, but now the claw foot furniture was sagging, the upholstery faded, the doilies and tasseled lampshades discolored, the folds of the heavy velvet curtains layered with dust. Pappy with his bare feet and undershirt almost fit in with the decor now. I smiled to myself and propped my feet on a flowered hassock.

"Where's your aunt?" I asked. "Is she home?"

"She died three months ago," he said.

"What happened...did she choke to death on all the dust in here?"

"Heart attack."

"Convenient for you."

"Ahhh, she was a nice old lady," he said, trying to scold me in his own timid way. "She left me the house."

"Like I said, convenient for you."

"The house is free and clear; all I have to do is pay the taxes."

"Looks like the place could use a little work."

"Yeh, I know," he said, looking apologetically at me with his cow eyes. The women loved those big, sad cow eyes of his. He actually was a handsome guy – dark features, a Roman nose, an even row of white teeth, olive skin – he looked more like a dago than a Greek. "I just haven't found the time. I'm on the road all the time."

"So you're driving a truck?"

"I work for Landstar....They're in Youngstown. The Prison Society gave me a referral when I got out of Marian, but they told me I needed a license, so I took a six week truck driving course and got my license."

"They pay you by the mile?" I asked, getting sick of the small talk.

"Yeh, thirty-four cents a mile."

"Thirty-four cents a mile," I repeated without interest.

"I can make a good buck, but it means a lot of driving; you have to cover the miles." I didn't give a flying fuck about his truck driving career, and he knew it. He was squirming around in his chair, and I heard the tension in his voice. He looked like a guy who knew he was going to get blindsided; he just didn't know from which direction. "How did you find me?" he asked cautiously.

"The Prison Society. I told them I was your brother." Pappy stiffened in his chair. "They were very helpful. They told me where you worked, and the trucking company told me where you lived, and here I am."

"Here you are," he stood up and sat right back down again, sending up a cloud of dust particles from the chair cushion that enveloped him in the light from the table lamp. "What do you want, Prado?"

"I mentioned your brother. That's why I'm here – because of him."

"What do you have to do with my brother?"

"Have you talked to him lately?"

"I haven't talked to him in years – You know I don't even know where he's living now."

"He's living in Redvale, Pennsylvania. I ran into him at a baseball game. You know how I like baseball. The town has a minor league team. I thought he was you at first."

"Did you talk to him?"

I pulled a cigarette from the pack in my shirt pocket and took my time lighting it. "You got an ashtray?" I blew out the match and held it out to him. He got up from the chair and practically ran out of the room. He came back in a few seconds and handed me an empty coffee can. "No," I said, putting the can between my legs. "I didn't talk to him; I knew he wasn't you. He works in the cash office at the ballpark, if you're interested – I sure was."

Some of the color drained out of his face as he gripped the arms of the chair. "You still didn't tell me why you're here," he said nervously because he at least had an inkling now.

"Stand up," I told him.

"What?"

"Just stand up for a second, Pappy – I'll explain."

When he stood, I matched up the two brothers in my mind. A perfect match; all Pappy had to do was lose the mustache and get a haircut. They even weighed the same. Pappy might've been a couple pounds lighter.

"What's this all about, Prado?"

"Running into your brother gave me an idea."

"What kind of an idea?" I knew from looking at the pained expression on his face he knew my idea was against the law.

"You and I are going to rob the ballpark," I smiled.

He jumped up like the chair was on fire. "You're crazy."

"No I'm not. I've got it all figured out, and your brother is going to help us."

"My brother isn't going to help you rob any place."

"You'd be surprised what a person will do with the proper motivation." He stood there looking like he didn't know whether to spit or shit, his slightly pudgy body quivering around the edges.

"You...you can't be serious."

"Did you ever know me when I wasn't serious?" I took a deep drag on my cigarette and blew a smoke ring at him.

"I mean...you can't just come waltzing in here asking me to do something that's going to put me back in jail – and involve my brother, too."

"What do you mean, I can't? I just did."

"Listen, Prado," he said, which was the one thing I wouldn't do. "I'm off parole now. I'm free and clear and making decent money, and I want to keep it that way. I don't want any trouble – Do you understand, Prado?"

"Do I understand?" I said. Did a stone wall understand? I'd expected this reaction from him. His words just bounced off me.

All the weeping and wailing in the world wouldn't have touched me. He was wasting his breath, only he didn't know it, but he would when he realized the only thing I understood was I needed him for this job, so he was coming with me – walking or sliding – he was coming with me.

"Decent money," I sneered. "How many miles do you have to drive at thirty-four cents a mile to make a hundred grand, Pappy? How many miles? And your end of the take might be more."

"I don't even want to hear about it," he sat down again and seemed to brace himself in the chair. "I'm not interested. I'm sorry you wasted your time coming all this way to see me."

"I'm not wasting my time, you are."

"You can't make me help you....I mean what are you going to do...? You can't make me come in with you."

I put my cigarette out in the coffee can, got up and set the can on a claw foot lamp table with a mother-of-pearl inlay marked with coffee cup stains. "You're right. I can't make you do anything you don't want to do." I lit another cigarette and threw the match on the oriental carpet. "You're right, but remember my cellmate, Kutchie – Remember him? I wanted him to do something for me, and he wouldn't do it. I couldn't make him do it; I didn't try....You remember what happened to him in the machine shop – remember?"

I walked over and stood beside him. He kept his head down, but he rolled his eyes up to watch me. I put my hand on his shoulder, and he flinched. "Relax," I said and quickly moved my hand to the back of his neck and dug my fingers into the tendons. I had strong hands from gripping a baseball. "You're not the homemaker type, Pappy," I said as I squeezed. "You keep a very untidy house....This place is obviously too much for you; I'm going to take you away from all of this." When he dropped to his knees, I released my grip and he went on all fours on the floor, tears welling up in his eyes.

"For crissake," he struggled to his feet, rubbing the back of his neck. "What are you trying to do? Keep your hands off me....I can pick up that phone and have you back in Marion for a long time."

"You're not calling anyone except your boss," I slapped him on the back friendly like. "I'm going to help you out here. Just listen to me; I'm going to tell you exactly what to do." I put my arm around his shoulders and led him over to the phone and handed it to him. "You call your boss or whomever you have to call and tell him you have a family emergency; tell him there's a serious illness in the family, and you need a personal leave or whatever you want to call it until next Sunday – the 28th – You'll be back then – It's an emergency – Understand?"

"How can I come back?" he put the phone back on the hook. "You're not making any sense. You might be able to force my brother into helping you, but what's to stop him from talking afterwards? The cops will track me down in no time."

I didn't say anything; I didn't have to. His eyes got wide as the realization sunk in, and he put his hands out as if he was trying to fend something off, slowly wagging his head. "The way I have it figured, it puts you in the clear – no loose ends –"

"You're talking about my brother."

"It has to be this way, Pappy – Don't you see? Otherwise, everything falls apart afterwards. I'm telling you, it's perfect."

"He's my brother," Pappy said. He stepped back from me and almost fell over the coffee table.

"What's the matter with you? Didn't you tell me he was nothing to you now? It's been years since...You're practically strangers."

"He's still my brother; we grew up together."

"Don't give me that shit," I practically spit at him. "How many times did you tell me you hated him? How many times did you tell me he never stuck his neck out for you – not once? Hell, you and I spent more time in the can together at Marion than you have with him over the past fifteen, twenty years."

"I don't know...." The sweat was standing out on his olive skin in little silver beads.

"Maybe I can help you make up your mind," I said. "If I can't get your cooperation, I'm going to have to try to figure something else out – What, I don't know, but I do know it won't include you, and since I've already told you too much, I sure as hell can't afford to leave you behind to talk."

"Geezus, Prado...Geezus." He pulled his undershirt from his shorts and, stretching it up, used it to wipe his face.

"So make up your mind. Either you can do this job with me and go back to driving your truck a helluva lot richer than when you left, or I can make it look like you walked in here in the middle of a burglary and got your head caved in." I picked up the phone and started to dial the number of the trucking company. "What's it going to be? Make up your mind before I finish dialing this number."

He glanced at the front door and then back at me, and I just smiled and shook my head at him, knowing what he was thinking.

"All right," he said "All right... all right." I handed him the phone. He looked like he'd been sitting in the middle of a steam bath. He listened to the phone ring at the other end and then asked for the human resources department.

Pappy said all the right things, and the fear I'd put into his voice added just the right touch for the situation at hand. They wanted him to come into work to fill out a form, but he managed to convince them of the urgency of the situation, and they agreed to mail him the form if he returned it when he came back Sunday. After he talked to his supervisor for a minute, he said good-bye, and when I took the phone from him and hung it up, the earpiece was wet with sweat.

"What are you in a lather about?" I asked. "Relax – stop your sweating. You did good, Pappy...real good. Didn't I tell you there wouldn't be a problem?"

"Now what?"

"Now you go towel off and start packing because we're going to be traveling tonight. We've got a long drive ahead of us."

"To Redvale?"

"To Redvale...for a family reunion."

I kept my eye on him while he got dressed, packed a suitcase for the week, and locked up the house. He turned off the hall light, and we went out onto the porch. I'd forgotten how noisy it could get on a hot night in August in the country. The crickets were chirping like crazy, and the cicadas were droning away in the trees. He threw his suitcase in the back seat, and we got in the car. He didn't say a word for the first half hour of the drive back, which had to be a record for Pappy, and he still wasn't talking much when we crossed into PA. I waited until I hooked up with Interstate 76 on the other side of Pittsburgh before I started filling him in on all the details of the plan. By the time we got to the Bedford exit, and he took a turn behind the wheel to give me a break, he was droning on like one of those cicadas. After I'd laid out the job for him, I think he came to the realization if one brother can walk away with a hundred grand while the other brother gets deep-sixed, he'd rather be the brother walking away. They say blood is thicker than water, but when it's your blood getting spilled, sometimes it tends to run mighty thin. Then again – maybe Pappy, as I said, never gave a damn about his brother in the first place.

After we stopped for something to eat, I took the wheel again outside of Lancaster, and we reached Redvale at six in the morning. I got Pappy settled in my room at the River View and told him to shave the mustache before I came back, and then I'd take him for a haircut. When I walked into the office, Cocuzza presented a disgusting sight. He was bent over the front desk reading the morning paper while he stuffed his face with an egg sandwich. Bits of the sandwich were falling from his mouth and collecting on the paper. He hadn't even bothered to get dressed. He was still in his undershirt. I'd just gotten out of the car after an eight hour drive and on top of that the greasy burger I had eaten at the truck stop was laying in my stomach, and now the stomach acid was churning from looking at this disgusting bastard.

"I need a cot sent to my room," I said. "Someone's staying with me for a couple of days."

He didn't even bother to swallow what was in his mouth before answering me. "Waaa-nt ah c-ahhht...sho-r-r-wah." His open maw was filled with a partially chewed yellowish-white bolus he was trying to talk around.

"Have the kid bring it over right away," I said as I turned to leave.

"Ten dollar...that is ten dollar a night extra," he said, swallowing and clearing his throat. He wiped his mouth with the back of his hand.

"What are you talking about?"

"Sure...extra person in room is ten dollar a night."

"But my room is double occupancy."

"Have to bring cot in...that is extra – extra you see for cot."

Mark it down, I said to myself. Mark it down, Prado. If he wasn't on your shit list before, he is now. Someday – if the opportunity ever came up, I'd splinter this bastard's rib cage for him like I was stepping on a wicker basket.

"I understand," I said. I took two tens from my wallet and threw them on the desk, and the look I gave him almost made him gag on his next mouthful of sandwich. "Bring that cot over now." He nodded his head.

The kid who did maintenance work around the place rolled the cot up to the room door fifteen minutes later, and five minutes after that Pappy was sound asleep on it. I was exhausted, too, so I lay down intending to take an hour nap. I woke up six hours later. Pappy was still stretched out on the cot sleeping. He must've been dreaming because he twitched and jerked and a low moan came from his half-open mouth. It didn't appear to be a pleasant dream, so I did him a favor and kicked the side of the cot to wake him. He opened his eyes and looked at me without recognition and then closed his eyes again.

"Rise and shine, Pappy," I kicked the cot again. "Daddy is taking you for a haircut."

*****

I took my boy out of town for his haircut – way out of town. I found a small barbershop in an out of the way burg about ten miles south of the city. I told the barber exactly how I wanted him to cut Pappy's hair, and kept circling around the chair to make sure he was cutting it correctly. When we left, the barber looked at us like we were nuts, but I didn't care because Pappy walked out of there the mirror image of his brother.

We picked up some food and beer before we went back to the motel, and then I stashed Pappy in the room while I ran some errands. When I left him, he was hinting around about getting a woman, so I told him to sit tight and I'd fix him up later after I took care of some business. It was important he be kept out of sight until we were ready to move. We couldn't have two Papademetrious being seen around town, could we? That would never do.

I went over the bridge into Redvale and picked up a pair of sunglasses, a roll of duct tape, a duffel bag and a Redvale Phillies cap at a variety store, but I had a helluva time finding the fake beards I needed. There were no costume shops in the city and a couple of other ones only had hours during the Halloween season. I finally located a place open year round and bought a blank translucent mask and two adhesive beards.

By the time I got back to the motel it was dark. When I opened the door to my room, I heard the water running in the shower which must've pissed off the cockroaches who liked to sleep in the shower stall. I knew why Pappy was taking a shower; it wasn't for me. I ducked my head in the bathroom and yelled his name. He pulled the shower curtain aside and stuck out his head. His mop of hair was plastered over his forehead.

"What took you so long?"

"Where's your wallet?"

"What do you want my wallet for?" he sputtered.

"Hey, if you want it, you're paying for it."

"In my pants – hanging on the door."

I went through his pants pockets, found the wallet, and removed three twenties from it while he watched me. When I put the wallet back, he closed the shower curtain. It made me laugh... thinking about it – poor Pappy. I went looking for the kid and located him carrying a TV into a room in the other unit.

"My friend needs some company," I handed him the sixty bucks. "Room 112."

"If Mr. Cocuzza finds out –"

"What the hell are you talking about? This is between you and me. That old prick isn't going to find out about anything."

When I opened the door to the room, the smell of aftershave lotion hit me like a slap in the face. Pappy was standing in front of the bureau mirror running a comb through his hair and admiring himself. He was wearing dark dress slacks and a silky purple shirt.

"Well...?"

"She'll be here."

"You told him no niggers?"

"I told him," I lied. "Just keep off the bed – use the cot."

"Ahhh, hell the cot's too small," he said, looking at his hair from different angles in the mirror. "What's the matter? They'll change the sheets."

"Change the sheets – Where the hell do you think you are? They change the sheets once a week around this goddamned place. Stay off the bed – I mean it...I'm not laying in your slime."

Pappy walked over to the cot patting his hair with his fingers. He suddenly looked lost in thought. "I wonder what my brother's wife looks like?"

"I don't know," I said. "From what I could tell, she's got a nice build."

"Nice build, huhh?"

"What made you think about her just now, Pappy?"

He just shrugged and then sat on the cot. "A nigger better not show up at the door. I'll take a spic, but no nigger."

*****

The hooker showed up twenty minutes later. She was a dyed-blonde with black heels, a mini-skirt and some kind of sash top in the shape of an X – the top of the X covering her breasts. The big hoop earrings she was wearing banged against her face as she worked the gum in her mouth. I held up my finger giving Pappy the I'll be back in one hour sign and left.

I drove into West Redvale and stopped at the first bar I came to on Penn Avenue. It was a three-story brick row – the bar on the first floor and apartments on the other two floors. A mahogany bar with a cushioned lip ran the length of the place and took up most of the room. When I sat down, there was only one other guy at the bar. He was sitting at the far end drinking a beer and eating from a big basket of potato chips. After I ordered a shot of bourbon and a draft, I stared at myself in the bar mirror above the shelves of liquor bottles and thought about Pappy and the whore I'd gotten for him screwing on the cot at this very moment. It gave me a warm feeling inside knowing I could provide him with some enjoyment in the short time he had left on this earth. I gulped the shot of bourbon, and that gave me a warm feeling inside, too.

*****

Early the next day, I parked a block up from Papade-metriou's house on College Avenue and stayed there most of the morning. Nobody took notice of me because the college kids were pulling in and out for their classes all day. At quarter after eight, Pappy's brother left the house wearing a suit, so I figured the job at the ballpark was just a part-time or seasonal job. I passed the time watching the college kids playing tennis on the courts down the street and the kids strolling by the car with their backpacks and books.

At 10:45, the wife came out of the house dressed casually in sandals, shorts and a sleeveless ribbed top which showed off her big rack. She was a little hippy, but she slimmed down nicely below the waist to a pair of beautiful legs. Her dirty blond hair was pinned up in swirls on top of her head. She got into her car parked at the curb in front of the house. She made a left on Fourteenth Street and drove right past me. I'd already learned what I needed to know about her, but out of simple curiosity I followed her up the hill to Hampden Drive, made a left, and about a mile later she turned into the driveway of the Deer Trail Apartments tucked in the woods at the bottom of a steep hill. She parked at the far end of the lot shared by two brick-faced apartment buildings and knocked on the last door at the end of unit nearest the street. I had pulled in at the other end of the lot and decided to stick around until she came out. I waited close to an hour and a half before she came out. When she did, I noticed her dirty blond hair was unpinned and covering her shoulders. She took me back down the hill to the curb in front of her house, and that's where I left her.

When I got back to the motel, Pappy was sitting in front of the TV watching a game show with an unwrapped submarine sandwich on his lap and a can of beer in his hand.

"Where did that stuff come from?"

"I got the sandwich at a deli up on the avenue and the beer –"

I hit him with my open hand on the back of the head, and a little geyser of beer shot up through the tab hole in the beer can and wet his arm. "I told you stay put you dumb sonofabitch!"

"I got hungry. I was only out of the room a few minutes."

"Did anyone from the motel see you coming or going?"

"No."

"And what if someone saw you who knows your brother and wonders why you're buying a hoagie and a six-pack when you should be at work?"

"Nobody saw me," he said, wiping his arm across the front of his undershirt.

"How do you know?" I snapped. "What are you, invisible...? You're going to blow this whole deal before we ever get started – I'll tell you one thing – You're not sticking your nose outside this door until we move tomorrow. You stupid..." I caught myself. There was no point blowing up at him – making a tricky situation worse. I couldn't afford to beat up on him now. Everything depended on him and his brother; I needed him to think I was on his side.

"Sorry, Prado," he mumbled, looking at me like he was afraid I'd hit him.

"Forget it," I shrugged. "Just use your head next time, Pappy...Do you want me to get you some more beer when I go out to get something to eat?"

"Might as well."

"By the way," I added, "the wife's not bad – blond and built."

"You saw her." Pappy perked up. I could see his mind shifting gears.

"I saw her...a nice piece of tail – very nice." I left Pappy thinking about it while I went into the bathroom to take a piss. "I think she's doing somebody on the side," I called out to him. "I followed her to an apartment this morning, and she came out looking a little disheveled, if you know what I mean."

Pappy was licking his lips when I came back out. "What does she look like?"

"I'll tell you later. I have to get something to eat; I'm starving. I'll be back in about a half an hour."

I grabbed something to eat at a fast food place and then picked up a bag of ice, a couple of six-packs, and a bag of groceries and went back to the motel. I put the ice and beer in the sink, and then killed the rest of the day sitting in the room with Pappy listening to him yap while I tried to go over the details of the job again with him.

That night I got him another whore – a redhead this time, tall and skinny with big feet and a ton of makeup. I think he was already counting on another blond for the following night.

Beware Of Greeks Bearing Gifts

On Thursday, the 25th, after buying a big bouquet of flowers at a florist shop in West Redvale and two red short sleeve Redvale Phillies logo shirts and a Phillies carryall at the ballpark souvenir stand when the gates opened, I returned to the River View Motel and checked out at quarter after six. Pappy had already put the bags in the trunk and was waiting in the car. He was wearing his new Phillies shirt.

I drove over the Wilson Street Bypass, took the Fifth Street exit, and checked the house to make sure the wife's car was there and the other car wasn't, and then stopped at the donut shop across from the high school baseball field. After I went in for coffee and donuts, I parked the car in one of the big mall lots on the Fifth Street Highway, and we sat there until it got dark.

*****

I parked the car across the street from the house. It wasn't pitch dark, but it was dark enough. The vapor street light on the corner blinked on and then faded out again. I took the two .38's and the roll of duct tape out of the glove compartment. Pappy stuck the .38 in one pocket and the tape in the other, and then reached back for the bouquet of flowers on the back seat. I could tell by the look on his face he was scared as hell. He'd gotten more quiet as the day went on and now he sat holding the flowers between his legs with both hands, and in the darkness of the car, I saw the sweat forming on his upper lip. I needed to give him a pep talk like a manager would give a rookie pitcher before his first start.

"You know what to do, Pappy," I said to him as I slipped the .38 under my belt, "but let's go over it again just to be sure."

"When she opens the door, I keep the flowers between me and her."

"That's right...keep your face partly covered. She's going to be surprised, so tell her you left early because you were feeling a little under the weather and decided to pick up some flowers for her on the way home, but tell her as you're going in the door – Get in that door even if you have to push past her, and give her the flowers right away so her hands are occupied."

"I hope I don't have to belt her."

"That's up to her. She might not be able to tell you from your brother, but she's married to the guy.... Something might tip her – If not, when you pull the gun on her, that might set her off. Either way, if she opens her mouth, you have to shut it quick – one way or another."

He wiped his mouth with the back of his hand. "I just want to get this over with," he said, reaching for the door.

I grabbed his arm and leaned so close to him I could smell the jelly donut on his breath. "Hold it a second," I said. "Just take it easy...do what I told you and everything will go fine, and remember to give me the signal at the door when you get her settled down.... Now, go ahead, and remember – keep her under control when you get in there."

I rolled down the window and watched him cross the street holding the flowers in front of him. He went up the steps and peeked in the window before ringing the doorbell. He stood shifting his weight back and forth nervously from one foot to another, holding the flowers in front of his face. The door finally opened, and I heard him say, "surprise" in a weak voice. The wife said something I couldn't understand as he pushed past her into the house. The door closed, and I braced for the fireworks, but from where I was sitting I couldn't hear a peep coming from inside the house, which was a good sign, so I waited for Pappy's signal at the door. I waited and waited, and five minutes later I was ready to move without the signal when the door opened and

Pappy waved me in. I casually crossed the street, and when I entered the house, I saw her sitting on the sofa with her hands taped behind her back and a piece of tape covering her mouth. Her hair was wet and she was wearing a purple robe and slippers. The position of her arms had pulled the lapels of the bathrobe open showing off her cans. I walked past her through the house to the kitchen. The kitchen door was hanging open. I closed and locked it, and then closed all the curtains on the first floor.

"Check the upstairs," I told Pappy. His .38 was on the coffee table. "Take this with you, stupid." I slapped the gun into his open palm. "– And don't touch anything except the doorknobs." The wife's eyes followed him up the open staircase and then focused on me. Petals from the bouquet lying in the middle of the living room were scattered over the carpet.

"This ain't your day, is it?" I winked. "Sorry if we interrupted your shower." I stepped around the coffee table, and she tried to squirm away from my reach. "Relax," I grabbed the lapels of her robe and closed them, tucking them under her chin. "Now that's better....We can't have your brother-in-law getting himself too keyed up – not yet anyway."

Pappy came loping down the steps. "Nothing," he said.

"No kids, huh?" She shook her head no. I sat on the edge of the coffee table so her knees were between mine. "I'll take the tape off your mouth if you promise to be quiet." I made a fist and brushed her cheek with my knuckles. "But if you start screaming..." I loosened a corner of the tape with my fingernail and slowly peeled the tape off her mouth while Pappy gave her a hard look, examining her from head to toe. She had a low, smooth forehead under her mussed up blond hair, high cheekbones sprinkled with freckles, a sharp, upturned nose, and thin, colorless lips that gave a cold expression to her face. But the first thing you noticed about her face was the eyes.

"I'd almost forgotten my husband had a brother," she said, regarding Pappy. Then she fixed her eyes on me, and I realized the coldness in her expression came from her eyes, not from the severe line of her mouth. Her eyes had turned to blue quartz as she stared at me – cold and shiny – and where there should've been fear, there was only contempt. "And if you're hanging around him," she said to me, "you must be as big a bum as he is. What do you two want? There's no money here."

I won't have to worry about this one falling into hysterics, I thought – not this girl. "You speak right up, don't you?" I put the balled up piece of tape in my shirt pocket, stood up, and yanked her to her feet by the arm. "The less you know about what we want, the better off you'll be, so no more questions. You just do as you're told and you'll be fine. When do you expect your husband tonight?"

"Around twelve."

"I look forward to meeting him."

"You're wasting your time. You're not getting any money out of my husband."

"Thanks for the advice." I led her over to the stairway and shoved her down on the steps. "I'm going to take the tape off your wrists, and then we're going upstairs –"

"You rotten bastard, what are you going to do now, rape me?"

"Not him," Pappy smiled. "But don't give me any ideas."

"Shut up," I told Pappy. "As for you...stand up and turn around.... I'm not your husband," I said as I unwrapped her wrists, "and I'm not your boyfriend." She gave me a surprised look. "Just remember that the next time you open your mouth to me if you want to stay alive – now move!"

I left the bathroom door partly open and waited for her outside in the hallway while she got dressed. When she was dressed, I made her pack a suitcase for herself and another suitcase with some linens, towels, and toiletries before putting coffee, bread and food from the refrigerator for sandwiches in a paper bag. Pappy transferred his suitcase to the trunk of her car and then brought it around to the alleyway behind the house and put the two suitcases in the trunk. When he came back to the house, I had him tape her wrists behind her back again. I tore off a short strip for her mouth.

"I'll take this off when we get in the car." Those ice cold blue eyes of hers were boring a hole in me – seeming to take the measure of me. I would do the driving and let her sit in the back sit with Pappy so I wouldn't have to look at her face.

"Where are you taking me?"

"I told you, no questions, but since you asked...we're going on a camping trip. Now let me ask you a question. Did you know he wasn't your husband right away?"

"It's impossible to tell them apart."

"But you knew right away, didn't you?"

"As soon as I got a good look at his eyes. There's something about his eyes."

I pressed the tape to her mouth. "Something about the eyes, huh?"

"I'll drive, Pappy."

Pappy led her out to the car and got in the back seat with her while I turned out the lights. I left the kitchen door unlocked.

*****

The drive to the cabin took about forty minutes. Pappy took the tape off her mouth, and she started right in grinding away and asking questions, so to keep myself from having to reach around and crack her in the mouth, I told Pappy to put the tape back on.

We reached the cabin just before ten. It was pitch black except for a lamp post at the foot of the driveway. When we passed the other cabin closer to the lake, I didn't see any cars parked in front of it, so we'd have complete privacy if they had remembered to leave the key on the ledge above the door. If the key wasn't there, I had a big problem on my hands. I went up on the plank porch with the wife while Pappy got the bags out of the trunk. The key was above the door just as promised, along with a spare. I opened the door and turned on the lights. There was a sheen to the whole place from the polished pine paneling and furniture. As soon as Pappy put down the suitcases, I told him to make sure all the windows were locked and to close all the curtains. The cabin was stuffy as hell with the windows closed, but we'd just have to sweat.

There were two bedrooms – one had a double bed and the other had bunk beds. I put her suitcase in the bedroom with the bunk beds. "You got the bottom bunk," I told her as I peeled the tape from her mouth again. "Your brother-in-law has the top bunk. Those are the sleeping arrangements."

"What is this?" she started firing questions as soon as the tape was off. "Why am I here? Are you holding me for ransom? I told you, my husband doesn't have any money – " I hit her on the jaw with the back of my hand, but it still knocked her cold. I picked her up from the floor and dumped her in the lower bunk.

Pappy came into the bedroom with his suitcase and saw her curled up on the bunk bed. "What happened?" he asked as he checked the window. "What'd you do to her?"

"She's all right. I just got tired of her yapping." He sat down on his suitcase and looked at her. The wheels were turning in his head as he looked her over. He was getting himself all charged up. "Keep your stuff in the other bedroom."

"I thought me and her were sharing a bedroom."

"You are – you're going to be bunk mates. Just keep your stuff in the other room. Give me the handcuffs."

Pappy rummaged through his suitcase, found the cuffs, and handed them to me. I cut the tape off her wrists with my pocket knife. She made a soft mewing noise, her eyelids fluttering. Pappy watched with keen anticipation as I cuffed her to the metal bed frame.

"I was thinking, Prado –"

"Don't use my name, stupid."

His brother's wife moaned, took a deep breath and opened her eyes. She looked at us groggily. I motioned for Pappy to leave the bedroom, and I followed him out and closed the door behind me.

"Anyway, I was thinking...since she won't be doing any talking...what difference does it make? I mean what difference does it make if –"

"What difference does it make if you grab some ass? None...except if you forget to keep your mind on business – I didn't bring you in on this so you could have a romantic getaway with your brother's wife. Keep your hands off. You let your dick screw up this job, and I'll –"

"I understand. You don't have to worry about me."

"That one in there is trouble – big trouble. I could tell that the first time she opened her big mouth. Your brother must have his hands full with this bitch."

"She's going to have her hands full with me."

"You keep her cuffed to the bed frame except when she has to go to the bathroom. When she's out of the cuffs be sure to stick to her like glue – like glue. Don't turn your back on her for a second, and if she starts yapping, tape her mouth – in fact it's probably a good idea to keep her mouth taped all the time."

I opened the door, and we went back into the bedroom.

"I'll stick to her, all right," Pappy said as he sat on the bed next to her. He stroked her bare thigh below the line of her shorts. "Don't worry, I'll keep her occupied. She won't have time to cause any trouble – Ain't that right, honey?"

"What are you...what happened?" She was staring at him with a blank expression. The fog was slowly lifting.

"If you don't have any questions," I said, "I'll get going. Just handle everything like we talked about. I don't want any problems. I'll be back about ten in the morning."

"You bring anything to drink?"

"No – listen to me Pappy. I better not walk into any problems tomorrow morning. I mean it...if you screw this up, they'll find you floating belly up in the lake down the road."

"Don't worry, I'll take care of everything at this end."

"I'm taking the spare key with me. I'll see you tomorrow."

"Did you bring anything to drink?" he persisted.

"Alcohol is prohibited on the grounds. We wouldn't want to break any park laws, would we?"

She tried to sit up but found she could not because she was handcuffed to the bed. "It's all right, honey," Pappy practically cooed as he caressed her cheek. "No one's hurting you again – not while I'm here."

She struggled in her cuffs. Her head had cleared and she knew where she was and who he was.

"Relax," he said. "You'll hurt your wrists. Just pretend I'm your husband. It shouldn't be too hard. Spiro and me are the same in every way – except in one department, and you'll be glad to know I'm a lot bigger in that department."

She would've slapped him in the mouth. I could tell she wanted to at that moment more than anything in the world, but her hands were cuffed, so she whipped her legs around and tried to knee him in the belly. He blocked her knees with his forearm and then draped himself across her body and held her down on the bed. She struggled helplessly under his weight as he laughed at her. "You disgusting piece of garbage," she said and then lifted her head and did the next best thing – spit in his face. On that note, I left the lovebirds alone.

On the drive back to the city, I thought about the lake and made a mental note to pick up a shovel when I got the baker's apron and hat. I wasn't going to mess around trying to weigh down a body. I'd find a quiet spot for Pappy in the woods behind the cabin.

The Bean Counter

It was 11:15 when I got back to the house. I wiped off every-thing we might've touched, even remembering to flush the Cello-phane wrapper the bouquet of flowers came with down the toilet. Then I waited in the living room with the .38 on my lap for the sound of a key turning in a lock.

At 12:20, Spyridon Papademetriou came in, saw me sitting on the sofa, and froze while his brain processed every conceivable reason for me to be sitting on the sofa in his house after midnight pointing a gun at him. "What are you doing here?" he gave up. "What the hell is this?"

"You'll get a lot more sleep tonight if you let me ask the questions," I motioned with my gun hand for him to sit in the armchair across from me. "Now if you'll just sit down...."

"Where's my wife?"

I didn't answer him; I was looking at his eyes. His wife was right; it was something about the eyes. Something in them or not in them; I couldn't be sure which. But that could be remedied easily enough.

"Is she here? Where's my wife?"

"You and your wife must have a hard time communicating. You both want to ask questions when you should be answering them."

"Where's my wife?" He was getting frantic.

"She's not here."

"Where is she?"

"Someplace else."

"Is she all right? God...you haven't hurt her?"

"Not a hair on her head," I answered. "She's in loving hands as we speak." My patience had worn razor thin. I was tired. It was late, and I was as tired of this Papademetriou brother as I was of the one back at the cabin, and this one had just walked in the door.

"...Is this a robbery?" he droned on. "I don't keep money in the house."

"Enough!" I jumped up. "Shut your goddamned mouth before I come over there and step on you. I'll tell you when to talk; until then, shut up and listen.... Now do I have your undivided attention...?"

He lowered his head. His mouth was working, but he said nothing. There was torment in his face, and it was bringing the sweat out on his forehead. He sweated just like his brother.

"Good," I said. "Now this is the way it's going to be. I'll tell you what I know, and then I'm going to ask you questions about what I don't know, and you're going to give me the answers – real simple – Right...?"

"Right."

"I know you work in the cash room at the ballpark; I know we're going to rob the cash room this Saturday; I know you're going to help us, and I know one more thing. If you don't help us – If we don't get your full and complete cooperation, you'll never see your wife again – alive that is."

"Please...don't hurt her." His lips were trembling like he was ready to cry.

"She won't get hurt if you cooperate."

"I'll cooperate, but I don't see how I can help you –"

"You'll see," I tucked the .38 under my belt and leaned back on the sofa. "Believe me, you'll see, but first things first. You work for the team part-time?"

"Yes, during the season," he answered, dabbing his forehead with a crumpled tissue he'd pulled out of his pocket. "My full-time job is with Ross Rosemont and Company. It's an accounting firm in Redvale."

"An accountant, huh?" He didn't answer; he'd noticed the bouquet of flowers I'd thrown on a console table, and the confusion over how they fit into the grand scheme of things was all over his face. "I knew a lot of former accountants and auditors in prison – some of the biggest crooks I've known. Subtract an entry here, add an entry there, and all of a sudden you've made yourself a pile of money – You know how it works. Nice and neat – not like sticking a gun in a guy's face and taking his wallet." He was done looking at the flowers, but he was still sweating while he waited for me to go on. "What hours will you be working at the ballpark tomorrow and Saturday?"

"I go in tomorrow at six and I'll probably get home about the same time as tonight. Saturday's a twilight double-header, so I'll go in at five, but I'm not sure when I'll get home because – " He stopped and looked at me, realizing the implication of what he'd said.

"You work a lot of hours between your two jobs. Does your wife work?"

"No, she doesn't."

"She doesn't have any kids to watch?"

"No, we don't have any children."

"So what does she do to fill her day?"

"What do you mean?"

"I mean does she sit here all day and keep the home fires going while you're out – " I caught myself before I went any further. Stupid, I thought to myself. I'd be cutting my own throat if I continued down that road. "Nothing...never mind," I said. "How many other people will be working in the cash room Saturday?"

"Three or four other people besides me...and the security guard."

"Is he armed?"

"Yes, he's armed, and he controls the access to the cash room."

"Tell me about the security system."

"It's a closed system – like the convenience stores have – four surveillance cameras. It's set up more to watch the employees, not to catch anyone on tape breaking in. The cameras re-loop every twenty-four hours. That way, they can scan the tapes if the cash counts don't come out or the safe is short to check on the employees."

"How much cash do they keep in the safe?"

"Between fifty and seventy-five thousand."

"Do you have the combination?"

"No, only the one full-timer has the combination, but the safe is left open during the hours I'm there."

"Very good," I smiled benevolently. "You're doing fine...just fine"

"What about my wife? You say she's all right; can I talk to her?"

"When the time comes, you can talk to her," I said, my benevolence turning to annoyance. "How's the office laid out?"

"The safe is in one corner and a coin sorting machine and cash wrapping machine in another corner of the room. The security guard's station is just inside the door, and there are two cash counting tables parallel to each other in the middle of the room. That's about it."

"No bathroom?"

"No, we have to use the one in the concourse."

"Any manual alarms or stab alarms?"

"Just one on the inside door connected to the alarm company. If someone tries to open the door improperly or force it, the alarm is triggered, and the police are contacted by the company."

"Any other way to get inside the room other than that set of doors?"

"I need something to drink," he said. He was licking his lips. "My mouth is dry."

"Sure," I said. "Go out to the kitchen and get yourself a drink." He stood up and waited for me, expecting me to follow him into the kitchen with the gun at his back. I put my feet up on the coffee table and my hands behind my head. "Well, go ahead – just remember what I told you about your wife's health depending on your full cooperation before you get any ideas about bolting out the back door." I heard the water running in the kitchen sink and a cabinet door close, and then he came back into the living room holding a glass of water. There was a tidal wave of fear and frustration dammed up behind his eyes. "It all comes down to trust," I told him as he took a sip of water. "I have to be able to trust you, and you have to be able to trust me."

"Why should I trust you?" he asked. "I could do everything you say, and you still might kill my wife."

"Because you have no choice, just like I have no choice.... Now what were you saying about another way into the office?"

"There is no other way in except through the two doors."

"How do those doors work?"

"An employee who's authorized punches in a security code on the first door," he said, pausing to take sips of water. That triggers a buzzer on the inside door to let the guard know someone's coming in.... The guy steps into the corridor, but even when the guard sees it's someone who has a right to come in, he can't open the second door. The second door won't open, can't open, until the first door locks behind the guy in the corridor.... That means the guy is trapped in that corridor. He can't go back because the first door is locked and he can't go through the second door until the guard sees everything is okay and opens the door.... It doesn't matter if you get through the first door because you can't force your way through the second door and you can't make the guard open it. The door is made of steel, three inches thick with bullet proof glass —"

"How does the guard open the doors?"

"There's a button he presses on the wall that unlocks the door to the concourse. The inside door works by compressed air. He pulls down a lever set in the door to open it."

Nothing had come out of his mouth that I hadn't already taken into consideration. "When would you expect the collected take from the games to be transferred to the cash room for counting Saturday night?" I asked.

"We'll have all the ticket money counted by the middle of the second game," he said. "The parking and concession money starts coming in for tabulation and counting at the end of the game. Usually all the cash has been removed to the cash room by the time security has cleared the ballpark."

"You mean the guys in the yellow shirts?"

"That's right," he stood up and lunged forward, his head wagging back and forth. "I don't know what you're thinking," he said desperately, but whatever it is, it won't work. There's no way you can get into that room, and if you think I can get you in, you're crazy. The guard outweighs me by fifty pounds; the first wrong move I made, he'd be all over me – not to mention the other guys in the room. I'd need a weapon, but something I didn't tell you is the guard scans us with one of those electronic wands when we first come in – every night. He even scans Mike, the full-timer, every night and makes him empty his pockets, and Mike has worked there fifteen years. I'm telling you –"

"You're telling me?" I gave him a smile steeped in wisdom. "You're not even going to be in the room."

"I'm not going to be in the room?" he looked at me in total confusion. "What are you talking about? I don't understand. Then how –?"

"All will be revealed, but first there's a couple more questions I want to ask you, so sit down and relax."

"I don't know what you're planning –"

"You know exactly what I'm planning; you just don't know how the plan can succeed, but you will when I say two words to you. Now sit down and tell me about your job – what it is you do when you're there...you're work routine?"

"Well...we take in the receipts from the designated cash collection points and also open up mail. Then all the cash collected must be balanced daily by comparing the total cash, checks, credit card receipts...to the register totals, ticket window totals, pre-numbered receipts, and money received in the mail. Any discrepancies have to be investigated and resolved. The entire amount of receipts collected must be prepared for deposit so that all receipts are posted as receipts to the club accounts. Then the deposit is secured in the safe until it is picked up by the armored car service for the bank.

"When does the armored car make the pick up?"

"The next morning – then we have to verify the processing of the transactions to make sure that all the transactions are complete, authorized, recorded, and deposited on time."

"It's all very general.... I'm not sure –"

"There's no point going into detail about all the internal controls and policies," he said. "It wouldn't mean anything to you."

I rubbed my bleary eyes, exhausted from the long day that was still unfolding long after midnight. I was ready for sleep. I wondered if Pappy was in dreamland by now; the odds were highly against it considering what was in the bunk below him. His brother wasn't ready for sleep. His weight was poised on the edge of the armchair, his dark eyes as wide and bright as a rabbit's. "All right," I said. "Let me get to this from a different direction. Can you train somebody in a short period of time to fill in for you – to cover for you for a half hour or so?"

"I don't understand," he said. "I don't see the point –"

"Ohh, you stupid sonofabitch," I snarled. "Just answer me. Can you teach somebody in a day to cover for you – to fake it for a half hour to an hour if he memorized the layout of the room – where everything was – and who you worked with? Can you teach him one small part of your job – every detail of one small part of your job – enough so he could get by and cover for you?"

"Teach who?" he asked.

"Can you do it? Can you do it?"

"I suppose so if he just stuck to one thing. It would be simple enough if he took over for me and continued what I'd told him how to do."

"One more thing," I said, "tomorrow morning I want you to call in sick to work. Tell them your eyes are bothering you, and you have to see an eye doctor." I stretched out on the sofa and rested my head on a throw pillow. "I think I'll sleep right here tonight. You better go up to bed and get some rest; you've got a busy day in front of you tomorrow."

"You expect me to sleep after all you've told me – when I don't know if my wife is alive or dead?"

"Your wife is fine, and I'll let you talk to her when the time's right." I turned off the light on the end table, slipped off my shoes, and let them drop on the floor.

"Now go to bed."

"I don't believe this is happening," he said as he started to trudge up the dark staircase. "It's all so ridiculous; none of it makes any sense."

I propped myself up on my elbow. "I wish I could be at the family reunion tomorrow."

"What family reunion?" He leaned over the banister looking down at me.

"Who do you think is with your wife?" It still didn't register with him. "He's going to be spending the day with you tomorrow.... Remember I told you two words would explain a lot to you – clear up all the confusion. These are the two words – " He was bolting down the steps before I got the words out of my mouth, "...Your brother"

"I should've known," he cried. "I should've known he was involved in this. That no good – " His eyebrows went up and slowly anger came into his face. He switched on the table lamp and stood over me. The beads of sweat still clung to the bridge of his nose. "He better not touch her," he said.

"Nobody's going to lay a finger on her if you do like you're told."

"You tell him he better leave her alone," he went on, his cheeks puffed in rage.

"You tell him. You're going to see him tomorrow."

"He's no good; he's never been anything but trouble – his whole life – nothing but trouble. I swear if he touches her I'll kill him."

"You've got things a little turned around, haven't you?" I turned off the light again. "Just calm down...I told you nobody's going to touch her as long as you cooperate. It's very late. Why don't you get some sleep? I can't have worry lines sprouting on your face.... Well, go ahead."

"My God...my God," he whispered lifelessly, blinking his eyes in disbelief.

"And don't think I don't know what's been running through your mind all night," I smiled at him. "And you're absolutely right. You could use the phone in the bedroom to call the cops. Hell, you could jump out the bedroom window tonight, and I'd never know, and tomorrow you'll have a hundred chances to yell for the cops; you could have them put a tail on me. Your brother and me would probably wind up back in jail – which would bother me less than you think because I've spent a lot of time in jail, and you get used to it, but you'd never see your wife again – except in pieces. I'd make sure of that, even if it meant my own neck. The first thing that gets done if cops show up on our doorstep – the very first thing would be to cut her throat."

His face froze, and I heard the hiss of air being sucked through his clenched teeth. "Please," he begged.

"I saw a guy in prison get his throat cut," I poured it on. "It's like drowning, only there's air all around you. You just can't get any of it into your lungs. You're gasping and gargling for breath, and it takes longer than you'd think to die.... That's the first thing I'd do, and after that if I had time, I'd really go to work on her to give you a lot of bad things to remember for the rest of your life."

"Please...don't hurt her," he whimpered. He looked like he was going to be sick to his stomach. It disgusted me to look at him. I knew exactly what I would've done in his place, but all he could do was stand there like a simpering worm. The miserable bean counter; all money meant to him were figures on a piece of paper. At least his brother knew sometimes you just had to reach out and grab things for yourself and not give a fuck about consequences.

"Ple-e-e-ease," I mocked him. "Don't say please to me. Who the hell do you think you're talking to? You disgust me on general principle, you know that? No wonder your – " I caught myself and returned to making my point. "It's real simple," I said. "I'm giving you a choice, a clear-cut choice. You can cooperate with us and you'll get your wife back unharmed and the ball club will be out some money, or you can double-cross us and the ball club will get to keep its money, and they might even kick in a few bucks to help pay for your wife's funeral – if they find enough of her to bury. Those are your two choices, you have no other options – Understand?"

"Yes...I understand."

"Good...and if you're worried about being implicated in this by the cops, there's no way that will happen when they find out your wife was kidnapped to force your cooperation. After they've satisfied themselves questioning you, they'll pat you on the back and send you back to your wife and you two can resume your miserable, mundane lives."

He didn't say a word; he'd come to a full appreciation of his situation. He turned away from me and started back up the steps to his bedroom; only this time it looked like he had a baby grand strapped to his bowed shoulders. I knew he didn't believe I wouldn't hurt his wife if he cooperated, but I also knew he didn't believe it enough not to cooperate.

"One more question," I called after him. "How much money do you calculate will be in the cash room at the end of the night Saturday?"

He kept slugging up the stairs as he answered, not bothering to look at me. "I don't know...considering it's a twin bill...maybe 150 - 160 grand including the safe money."

"160 grand," I whistled.

I listened to his steps in the hallway. When I heard a door close, I tucked the .38 under the sofa cushion, put my head back on the pillow and closed my eyes. 160 grand split one way, I thought – my way. Thinking about it was almost enough to make me start sweating.

The Fertile Crescent

When I woke up, Pappy's brother was talking on the phone, explaining to the person on the other end why he wouldn't be coming into work, going into some detail about his eye condition and his doctor's appointment before hanging up.

I sat up, took the .38 from under the cushion, and put my feet on the coffee table. "I see you're still here."

"I'm here." His face was drawn and his eyes were a bleary red, not from any eye condition, but from lack of sleep.

"Well, since you're still here, get me a cup of coffee – black. I take it that was Ross and whoever."

"That's right. You told me to call them, didn't you?"

"Good boy," I told him as he went into the kitchen.

When he came back into the room, the coffee cups were rattling on the saucers.

"Did you get any sleep last night? Christ, you look like shit. Why don't you take a nap after I leave because you've got a long day ahead of you?"

"I'll be all right."

"Before I forget, do you have sunglasses?"

"Yes."

"Wear them when you go to the ballpark tonight," I said. "Keep them on. If they ask you why you're wearing them, tell them the eye doctor gave you drops, and you have to keep them on for forty-eight hours."

"When is my brother coming here?"

I checked my watch. "You can figure on him getting here about eleven thirty – I don't want any trouble between you two. I want you to settle down to business. That's why I said you might as well try to get some sleep until he gets here."

"When can I talk to my wife?"

"Not today," I said. "You have too much to think about today. I want you to keep a clear head. You'll get yourself too keyed up talking to her."

"I want to talk to her today!" he shouted. He stared at me with narrow eyes filled with determination.

I regarded him evenly. "This is what happens when you don't get enough sleep," I broke into a smile. "Get a hold of yourself. I told you not today; tomorrow you can talk to her. Like I said, grab a nap after I leave. You're coming apart at the seams, and the day has just started."

The look of determination in his eyes had changed to exasperation. He sat down and balanced the coffee cup on his knee, but it started rattling again because his leg was trembling, so he set the cup on the floor. "What am I supposed to do when my brother comes here?"

"I want you to go over in detail with him what you are going to be doing at the end of the night after the game. I want you to go over with him down to the smallest detail what you're going to be doing during that period of time."

"He'll never get away with it; he'll do something stupid to give himself away."

"Does anyone in the cash room know you have a twin brother?"

"They don't even know I have a brother," he said, shaking his head reflectively.

"So he'd have to really screw up to make them doubt their own eyes," I said. "But he's not going to do that because you're going to tell him exactly what he has to do and how to do it – down to the smallest detail. You're going to describe the room, so when he walks into it, he'll feel like he's been there a hundred times before. You're going to tell him the names of the other employees and what they look like – what kind of personalities they have so he feels like he knows them."

"How am I going to switch places with him?"

"That's the easy part. Your brother will explain all that to you. Tonight's the dry run. You just clue him in on everything he needs to know. It'll work. He's only taking your place for a half hour or so, and during that time they're going to be looking at a mirror image of you."

"They'll be looking at my brother," he said to himself, the cold contempt heavy in his words. Then to me, "Even if I cooperate and do exactly as you say, what makes you think he won't get cold feet or double-cross you to save his own skin? I haven't seen him in years, but reliability isn't one of his strong points."

"Ohh, his feet are probably blocks of ice as we speak," I answered assuredly. "As for double-crossing me, I'm sure it's crossed his mind more than once, but he'll do as he's told because he hasn't got the guts not to. He's knows they could throw me in the darkest, deepest hole, and I'd somehow reach out of it to carve him up. He'd never get a good night's sleep again. He'll do what he's told just like you'll do what you're told, and it has nothing to do with your wife; it comes down to guts."

"You're very sure of yourself."

I lit a cigarette and filled my lungs. "I'm sure about you two," I tilted my head back and directed a plume of smoke at the ceiling. "You and your brother have more in common than you think."

"We have nothing in common," he snapped, the anger flaring up in his dark eyes like stirred coals.

I was thinking they both let women use them when the phone rang, and damned if I didn't jump. It sounded as loud as a fire bell.

"Well, answer it," I told him. "And like they say in the movies, act natural." I sat smoking and listening to his end of the conversation.

"Hello, Lorraine."

"..."

"She's not here," he hesitated. "...She went up to New York to visit her mother for the weekend."

"..."

"Good news for her...?"

"…"

"It's all right. You can tell me."

"…"

"Are you sure?"

"…"

"I...I had no idea. It's...a complete surprise."

"…"

"The good news...yes, she probably wanted to be sure."

"…"

"I won't say a word. You won't get into any trouble. I won't let on."

"…"

"Monday morning is fine.… You call her then."

"…"

"I will...I will...Surprised? I'll act very surprised."

"…"

"Goodbye, Lorraine."

He didn't hang up the phone right away, and I heard the clicking at the other end of the line from the woman trying to clear it to make another call.

"Who was that?" I asked him.

"Lorraine...from Dr. Zygmunt's office."

He was looking distractedly at me, as if he was trying to do some fast figuring in that accountant's brain of his, but the numbers weren't adding up. Then his eyes widened, and the puzzlement on his face condensed into big drops of sweat below his hairline. "I'm tired," he said. "I have to get some rest; I can't think anymore.… I can't.… He didn't finish the sentence, letting his mouth hang open.

"Go ahead," I said. "Just remember your brother's coming over around eleven thirty. I won't see you again until tomorrow night, so just remember what I told you if you decide to get any cute ideas – One more thing, give me your wallet."

"Why do you want my wallet?"

"Just hand it over, and take the money out first. I don't want any of your money, just the ball club's." He pulled his wallet from his back pocket, took out the bills, and tossed it over to me.

After he went upstairs, I washed my cup and saucer, wiped clean any surfaces I might have touched, and then left by the back door and walked up the back alley to where I'd parked her car on Richmond Street, a block from the house.

*****

It took me under an hour to get a pick and shovel at a hardware store and a baker's apron and paper cap at a restaurant supply house. On the way to the cabin, I picked up a couple of bags of groceries at a supermarket along 422. Pappy heard the car pull into the gravel driveway and was waiting at the open door in his boxer shorts to greet me.

"Here," I handed him one of the grocery bags. "Any problems?"

"No problems; how about at your end?"

"Everything went fine." As I followed him into the kitchen, I noticed the door to the bedroom was closed. I put the bag of groceries on the kitchen counter. "Put this stuff away."

"How's my brother?"

"You can ask him when you see him. He's looking forward to seeing you again."

"I'll bet he is," he said. "Do you want some coffee?"

I didn't answer him as I walked over to the bedroom door and opened it. A rank, feral odor hung in the dark room, and it seemed to grow stronger as I stood there – the smell of sweat and body fluids and overheated emotions. I felt my stomach do a back flip, churning up the nausea. I gagged once and then held on to myself tight, tasting the bile in the back of my throat. I ran over to the window and pulled the curtains open. I didn't give a damn; I was going to throw up if I didn't get some fresh air. I flipped open the window and pushed my nose and mouth against the screen, my lips forming a circle, pulsating, sucking in the air from the outside like a fish sucking in water. The sunlight was pouring into the room along with the summer breeze. It was a bad and stupid mistake, I thought, as I pushed back the nausea with hungry breaths of air, to have given Pappy all this leeway. There was no place in this cold and reasoned plan for the slippery mindless rutting of animals, the stink of it, sexual energy stirring up superannuated emotions, raw emotions that could cut back against the grain of this job – a dull plane prying up problems like splinters. That damned Pappy – he couldn't wait to tell his brother how many times he'd screwed his wife, and then his brother would go berserk, and one of them would end up killing the other one, and come Sunday morning, I'd be waving a fond farewell to my money as the armored car drove away. The fresh air was peeling away the layers of odor in the room and dispersing them. I turned on the bedroom light and the wife was staring at me from the bottom bunk.

"You must have a weak stomach," she said hoarsely. She sounded like she'd been doing a lot of yelling.

"And you must have a strong one," I said. She'd been watching me the whole time I was in the room.

"Not strong enough."

I walked over to the bunk beds. She was lying on her back in the bottom bunk, cuffed to the headboard. Her blond hair was tangled, and she had the same dark circles under her eyes as her husband. There was also a purplish-colored mouse about the size of a thumbnail under one of her cold blue eyes. She was naked under the cotton blanket covering her. She kept staring at me, those cold accusing eyes boring right into me, and I had to look away, but not out of guilt – only disgust. It sickened me to picture Pappy with his boxer shorts and paunch and sweaty ardor pawing at her with his sausage fingers. Both of them sickened me. I opened her suitcase, took out her bathrobe, and threw it on the bunk.

"I'll take off your cuffs," I told her. "Just behave yourself. I don't want any trouble." I unlocked the handcuffs, and she sat up, keeping the blanket wrapped around her.

"Why don't you tell that to the pig out there?" She was sitting with her back to me, and when she reached for her robe, she let the blanket fall from her shoulders, and I saw the tan lines from her swimsuit before she slipped on her robe.

"He won't be giving you any more trouble. I'll see to that. He won't bother you again."

"A little late...don't you think?" she asked as she put her feet on the floor. She stood up and tightened her robe. "It's a little late...." The tears started to roll down her cheeks.

"Get what you need out of your suitcase and go in and take a shower. You can have some breakfast afterwards." She was sobbing and wiping her face with the sleeve of her robe as she rooted through the suitcase. I stepped out of the room and stood in the doorway; I didn't want to be caught up by her emotions. I wanted to steer clear. "Go ahead...take a shower for crissake."

She brushed past me, holding clothing and toiletries in her arms, her bare feet patting against the wood floor. "Sorry if I offend you," she cried. She was looking for the door to the bathroom when Pappy came out of the kitchen, still in his shorts, peeling one of the oranges I'd bought.

She gasped when she saw him, dropped what she was carrying at her feet, and lunged for him with her hands out. He managed to grab one wrist but the other hand got through and latched on to his hair. He dropped the orange, and it rolled across the floor as she kicked at him. One of the kicks hit home because he groaned and his knees sagged. He swung wildly, hitting her on the side of the face, but she wouldn't let go of his hair, so he went down with her to the floor. I moved in and got my leg between them and levered Pappy off her while I squeezed her wrist. She finally let go, and I dragged her away from him like a sack of cement. Pappy got to his knees, rubbing his head with one hand and holding his groin with the other, swearing at her while she swore back at him. She was flexing her jaw and shaking her hand to get the strands of his black hair from between her fingers. He stood up and started for her, still holding his groin, but I stepped in front of him, grabbed him around the neck, and guided him to a chair.

I turned and saw her headed for the front door, and she would've made it out the door if I hadn't locked and latched it. She didn't have time to open it before I hooked my arm around her neck, hauled her over to where she'd dropped her clothing, and deposited her on the floor. I took out my .38 and pointed it in turn at her and him.

"I should kill both of you," I seethed. "It would give me great pleasure right now to put a bullet in both your goddamned heads. I have half a mind to and then just walk away and say to hell with it." Of course, I didn't have half a mind to do it; it wasn't even on my mind. I was just mad at myself because this uproar of emotions, this expenditure of energy and motion toward no specific end, served no purpose. This pointless burst of violence was my fault – my mistake.

"She started it," Pappy whined like a schoolboy casting blame.

I couldn't help but smile. It would give me great pleasure to put a bullet in his head, but I'd have to forego that pleasure – for now. I put the .38 back in my pocket. "You," I pointed at her. "Pick up your stuff and get in that bathroom. If you don't want to take a shower – fine. You can stay filthy, but get dressed." She gathered her stuff from the floor and went into the bathroom. "And keep the door open; don't worry, I promise I won't peek – stay away from the window, too."

Pappy stood up grimacing, holding his knees together. "I'll bust her wide open," he said. He bent over stiffly at the waist to pick up the orange and resumed peeling it. This was the man on whom the entire plan hinged.

"You're not touching her again," I said. "From now on you stick strictly to business. I made one mistake; I'm not making another, and if I hear otherwise from her, you're the one who's going to get busted open."

We heard the shower come on and turned our attention to the bathroom door. "Why don't you try her on for size?" Pappy said. "She's probably better wet than dry, and she's damned good dry." I saw the bathrobe coming off but couldn't see her coming out of it. Then the bathrobe was on the floor and she was in the shower.

"Shut up and get dressed."

"You might surprise yourself."

"I don't have any surprises for myself; I haven't for a long time, but I'll have a surprise for you if don't stop wasting time and get dressed and get the hell over to your brother's house."

He went into the other bedroom and closed the door. I slid an armchair with a plaid cushion and polished pine armrests into a position where I could keep an eye on the bathroom and felt the bulge from his brother's wallet as I sat down. I pried it from my back pocket and opened it. It was a fat wallet full of cards: credit cards, business cards, insurance cards, library cards, registration cards along with the driver's license, social security card, ATM card, motor club card....

In the pocket for the bills was a pink piece of paper folded into a little square. It was a lab report from the Redvale Hospital to *Dr. Donald Reinhohl for patient: Spyridon Papademetriou.* There was a *Medical History* section with columns of questions checked yes or no and the date a physical was performed and a *Semen Analysis* section with numbers typed in under several categories:

Sperm count	10/mL
Motility	1.5
Shape	100 norm config.

Under that was a *Blood Tests* section with more numbers typed in under a *Hormone Level* column. At the bottom of the page was an *Other Tests* section completed in long hand which was hard to read because it had come through faintly on the patient copy – something about a *transrectal ultrasound* coming back negative and a *postejaculatory* something or other also coming back negative. There was more written in long hand I couldn't make out.

I re-folded the paper, put it back in the billfold, and thought nothing more of it; I had too much else on my mind. The wife turned off the shower, dried herself in the tub, and then stood behind the partly open door and dressed. When Pappy came out of the bedroom, I gave him one of the paper grocery bags and he put the fake beard, the Phillies shirt and cap and the sunglasses in it. I gave him his brother's wallet, and he gave me his after taking the cash out of it. The wife was blow-drying her hair in the mirror. She kept glancing out at us nervously.

"What are you going to do all day with her, play cards?" Pappy asked.

"Remember to get the security code to the door from him," I said, ignoring his question. "And don't forget to put on his watch and wedding ring when you make the switch – and his ID tag."

"Give me the car keys."

"Yeh, you better leave before she comes out of the bathroom." I threw him the car keys. "I wouldn't want you two to get into another cat fight."

"That bitch," he grabbed his crotch. "My balls still hurt."

"I don't have to tell you not to say a word to your brother about you and her. You're not that stupid, right?"

"Why would I?"

"Because you like to talk, Pappy, but don't talk about this – not a word. If he even gets a hint about you and his wife, he'll blow the lid on this job. Just stick to business and don't get into any personal stuff – And make sure you tell him I'll let him talk to her tomorrow – not until tomorrow – twelve noon tomorrow."

"Anything else?"

"Are you clear on everything? No questions before you go...?"

"Just one," he said. If something goes wrong tonight for whatever reason –"

"You already know the answer," I said, not letting him finish the question.

"I'm on my own."

"Don't feel bad, Pappy; you'll have a lot of company. Everybody's on their own, every day of their lives...good luck." I was smiling sweetly at him as he closed the door.

She was running a brush through her hair in front of the mirror. It was very soothing for some reason to watch her brush her hair after all the commotion. I watched her brush her hair and then pin it up on top of her head in an elaborate procedure, taking hair pins from her puckered mouth and placing them at strategic points in the waves of her hair.

When she came out of the bathroom, I cuffed her one hand to the metal bracket support on a leg of the kitchen table. She was wearing a sleeveless orange blouse, black Capri pants, no shoes or socks and no makeup. I made eggs sunny-side-up and toast for breakfast. She kept her eyes on her plate and didn't say a word as she ate. It was a nice, peaceful breakfast. I could hear birds chirping outside the kitchen window. Which reminded me, I'd have to remember to close and lock her bedroom window when I cuffed her to the bunk bed again. As I watched her delicately dip her buttered toast into an egg yolk, I was thinking about when and how I would kill her tomorrow. She was considerate enough not to once look up at me.

The Dress Rehearsal

After breakfast, she complained how tired she was, and since I was going to cuff her to the bunk anyway, I was happy to let her sleep. I read the newspaper and listened to the radio to pass the time. When I tired of that, I settled into my main pursuit, pacing the floor like a caged animal wondering about Pappy. It was killing me thinking about all the ways he could screw up. A minor point I imagined I'd failed to impress upon him would throw me into a mild panic, and then I'd have to calm myself down. Then another minor point would occur to me, and I'd fall into a fresh panic. Depending on him, as I've said before, went against the grain with me, but he was the fulcrum on which this job succeeded or failed. It got so bad, I started peeking into the bedroom to see if she was awake so I'd have somebody to talk to, somebody to take my mind off Pappy – common, appalling, pointless Pappy. Why couldn't he be the twin with the brains instead of the stupid one? Why did I have to cast my fate with that whoremaster? It was the waiting I couldn't stand – the goddamned waiting. I'd sooner wade into a roomful of lifers than wait for anything, and tomorrow was another day of waiting, but first I had to wait for Pappy to walk through the door tonight – if he ever did.

At three o'clock, I walked into the bedroom hoping she was awake. If she wasn't, I was going to wake her. I looked at her, and she opened her eyes and looked back at me. Her eyes were the color of blue agate in the dimness of the room.

Pappy would've had a big laugh. "Do you want to play some cards?" I asked. I cuffed her to the kitchen table again, and we played black jack. You had to put something up; you had to play for stakes, so we split up the change in my pockets and played for that. She had only one free hand, so I dealt the cards. I guess I was holding the cards in more ways than one. She was a head-strong player, which didn't surprise me. She'd go for broke and hit on sixteen or seventeen. I knew it was just a matter of time before she'd go for broke with me – try to soften me up and make her play, but she was bound to go bust. The cards were stacked against her and had been since the first second I set eyes on her husband at the ballpark. She started in on me between hands and kept it up between hits. I wasn't listening to her; I couldn't hear her. I was too far ahead of her. Whenever my eyes went up from the cards, she'd fix on me with her eyes, those cold eyes melting into warm, blue pools by the yearning for understanding, compassion – release.

"After my husband helps you," she was asking now, "are you going to let us go?"

"Yes," I told her. "I'm going to let both of you go. How many times to I have to tell you?"

"I don't believe you."

I dealt her a face card and put the deck on the table. I peeked at my hold card; it was a king with a ten showing. "I've told you if you two cooperate, I'll let you go.... Do you want a card?'

She picked up her cards, barely gave them a glance, and stared at me. The mouse under her eye had faded to a grayish hue. "We've never done anything to you."

"Do you want a card?" She held up a finger. I flipped her a card – seven of hearts. "I'm standing." She looked at the card and threw the other cards on the table. Twenty-two – bust! I turned over the king and shrugged. She pinched her bloodless lips together.

"What kind of person could kill two people in cold blood?"

"Who said anything about killing anybody?" I asked her as I shuffled the deck.

"We're witnesses."

"You wouldn't be the only ones."

"Your friend told me everything last night. He started drinking, and he told me all about your plan."

He must've found the pint of scotch in my suitcase, I thought. "So he told you," I started dealing the cards. "So what?"

"He told me your name. Prado...Your name is Prado. He told me because he knew I wouldn't be telling anyone else."

Good old Pappy, I wondered if his mouth would be still chattering like a set of novelty store teeth when I put him in the ground. It was going to be a pleasure to put a bullet in his thick skull. "Look at your cards."

"No," she insisted. "You look at me. Why won't you look at me?"

I looked at her and saw the waves of blond hair on top of her head and the whiteness of her face and the thin line of her mouth and the blue, blue, blue of her eyes. "I'm looking at you," I said absently. "I'm telling you for the last time I won't harm either of you if you cooperate."

"I don't understand what makes a man like you," she said. "You can calmly look me in the eyes.... If we promised not to talk...would it mean anything to you? Please...." A tear had welled up in the corner of her eye and hung suspended from her eyelash. I was concentrating on it.

"I guess the black jack game is over," I finally said, putting the cards back in the deck.

"What kind of person are you," the movement of her head sent the tear skimming down her cheek, "that we should have to suffer...? What did society do to you?"

It jolted me, this implication. A social determinist? I wondered. I was happy to answer her. "Society isn't to blame; society did nothing to me. I suffered no childhood trauma, no abuse. I endured no psychological deprivation – no deprivation of any kind. I come from a loving, nurturing family. I was given opportunities. I'm well educated – two and a half years of college. The man you see before you is here of his own free will."

"Everything has its causes; things don't just happen by magic."

Another jolt and this one sent me all the way back to a small room with a cracked linoleum floor and bare plaster walls and the silhouette of the guard standing just outside the frosted window of the door with Interview Room etched in it, and I was sitting at an metal table across from Dr. Stringfellow. He was holding a clip-board with a pencil tied to it and wearing the same white, short sleeve shirt, black tie, black pants and black wingtips. He had a round face, but his features came together in a cramped con-fluence, the blue eyes so close together they almost appeared crossed, his blond hair white under the harsh fluorescent lights. That phrase – everything has its causes – had sent me back. Dr. Stringfellow had referred to it as "causal attribution". He was referring to it now.

"...No accidents, nothing just happens without a cause. There is no unavoidable fate, no mystical free will," he pursed his lips between each sentence before proceeding. Each time he did it, something inside me stretched tighter. "All events or actions are lawful – based on universal cause and effect relationships between antecedents and outcomes...."

I'd heard it all before, or, rather I'd read it all before in the prison library.

Psychological
Self-Help
By Bernard Stringfellow, PH.D.

He was a determinist; all prison psychologists were deter-minists; otherwise, they wouldn't be prison psychologists.

"...The earth is governed by scientific laws; likewise, in human behavior, it is predictable, based on complex laws of behavior that people will seek love, that behavior proceeded by reward tends to be repeated, that frustration arouses a response, that unpleasant experiences tend to be suppressed or repressed, that – and this is pertinent to your case history – negative self-evaluations are related to low self-esteem –"

"So to you," I interrupted, "personal freedom and choice are antiquated notions. Where's the sense of personal responsibility in your catalog of psychological laws? It seems to me our system of punitive control of bad behavior is built on sound assumptions: The murderer deserves to die, the rapist should be punished, the drug dealer or habitual criminal like me should be locked up. I am morally responsible for my actions as a result of some innate trait or character flaw or intentional decision – free will, doctor."

I was waiting for the shadow of the guard to move off the frosted pane of the door, but I don't know why. The doctor was talking again, and there were knots inside my guts.

"This is your destructive internal critic talking," the doctor said patiently. "It is the source of your low self-esteem, your low self-concept. You dismiss yourself – You dismiss the exploration of your history, environment and thought processes by claiming responsibility for your immoral, criminal behavior."

"You're wrong. I like myself, hard as that may be for you to fathom; I have no trouble facing myself."

"Ahhh," he sighed, and the knots inside me drew tighter. "You like your preferred identity, your best self. This tidy, stable description of self doesn't fit reality. You have a self with many parts...."

He was on to Chapter Seven now – *Understanding Ourselves and Our Relationships*. Freud and Berne were quoted frequently; the doctor prescribed heavily to their theories. I was looking over his shoulder at the door. The silhouette could've been painted on the pane of glass.

"...Unquestionably it is very complex," his voice was rising and falling in a whining sing-song. Would he ever stop talking? "One way to look at it is to say, 'If I knew all the laws affecting you, I would understand you perfectly. I would understand that given your physical makeup, given the effects of past experiences and your memory of past experiences and how you view the present, I would behave exactly as you're behaving, no matter how bad or good.' If you can think of it in this way: All human actions and feelings are governed by psychological laws, then all behavior becomes acceptable because it's lawful. Thus, your behavior is the natural, inevitable outcome of existing causes...."

Did he understand what he was saying? He didn't understand me because the knots were so tight they were burning holes in my stomach. I wanted to move him to a nice safe corner of the room and explain myself to him.

"An attitude such as this leads logically to tolerance of yourself and others and all that has happened in your past."

Then he gave me the cockroach test: How would I respond to the unenviable task of eating a cockroach?

1. Cockroaches don't taste too bad.
2. I'm tough. I can eat anything because I'm adventurous.
3. I don't deserve anything better to eat than cockroaches.

"Number one," I answered. "I read your book – insensitive to my own cruelty and indifference to others."

"You're not being honest with yourself," he insisted. "A disappointing response. You have to search deeply for the internal critic. This is the reason for your low self-concept, your low self-efficacy, your sexual confusion. We've been over this before. You have to recognize your internal critic and realize what pain the critic can help you avoid and what pain the critic causes. When you do this, you'll be able to understand this amalgam of low self-esteem and confusion over your sexual proclivities and inadequacies you've created for yourself. Face up to yourself – Yes, challenge your internal critic, and then you'll be able to understand and accept the things that can't be changed and your permanent weaknesses."

I understood with crystal clarity, so when the shadow finally moved off the door, I leaned across the table and hit him in the throat. "The self is whatever you define it to be," I said as I grabbed him under the arms and slung him into the corner. He was on all fours watching me with his blue, blue eyes as I came toward him. I was fumbling with the button on my dungarees. Somehow he managed to make a squeaking noise like a mouse. Then he made a higher pitched squeak before I could kick him in the stomach. I felt the billy club pressing against my windpipe, so I elbowed the guard. He nailed me on the collarbone with his club, rattling me down to my prison issues, and I hit him twice in the face, sending him against the wall. He slid down the wall to a sitting position, his cap pushed forward over his eyes. I wanted to tell Dr. Stringfellow I didn't believe Freud's or Berne's theories on the parts of our personality – three parts and six parts respectively. I wanted to tell him I believed in one authentic self, one true self, and I was just trying to be myself, but more guards came in and stopped me. It didn't matter; he wasn't sitting across the table from me anymore. She was sitting across the table from me now watching me with her blue, blue eyes.

I shoved her and she fell on the floor, her hand still cuffed to the leg of the kitchen table. She got to her knees, and I stood over her unbuckling my belt.

"Well," she said. My hands dropped to my sides. "Wel-l-l-l-l..."

I un-cuffed her from the table and led her into the bedroom. She slid into the bottom bunk, and I cuffed her to the headboard. "I could tell the first time I looked at you," she said as she positioned herself on her back.

"What could you tell?"

She turned her head and stared up at me. "Do you want me to say it?"

No, I didn't want her to say it. She was going to be dead in twenty-four hours, but she still had the advantage on me. I walked out of the room, and slammed the door shut.

*****

I made TV dinners for supper. I ate first, and then I let her eat. She didn't talk; she knew I didn't want to hear from her. When she finished, I put her back in the bedroom. I didn't want any company. After supper, I put the Redvale Phillies game on the radio. The game served as background noise as I passed the time attempting to picture in endless variations what Pappy was doing. As different as each version was through the course of the game, they all came to the same conclusion: Pappy walking through the front door.

I turned off the game in the middle of the eighth inning when she hollered to go to the bathroom the first time. I took off the cuffs and walked her to the bathroom and back. The second time she started in with the apologizing and pleading and promising she wouldn't say a word, talking very fast, the tears coming faster, throwing herself on my mercy, failing to comprehend that would have the opposite effect on me. She was too smart and knew too much to be placated, so she was reaching the inevitable verge of hysteria. Night had brought it on – the darkness settling in her room, the odd silence that made your ears hum. It was easier to hold on to some hope in the daylight; in the night, it tended to slip away to a dark corner and leave you alone. Tomorrow the hysteria would be full blown. The phone call to her husband tomorrow was going to be an adventure. It had to be made; I knew the husband needed it as an impetus, but I'd have to think through the logistics of the call very carefully.

I heard her in the bedroom carrying on, and I told her to shut up, but she kept it up until I got sick of listening to her and taped her mouth. It wasn't easy. She was kicking and biting, but I finally got the tape on. I'd already made up my mind about one thing; I was going to kill her after she made the phone call. She kept trying to talk with the tape on her mouth, but the words all came out like mush. When she finally settled down, I turned off all the lights, opened the front curtains a crack, and stationed myself at the window to wait for Pappy. I had a clear view of the stretch of road in front of the cabin. I set the .38 on the windowsill and smoked the last cigarette in the pack.

*****

At twelve-thirty, I saw the faint glimmer of headlights coming up the road from the lake. It was the first car I had seen on the road. The headlights came closer, and then the car slowed around a curve, the lights sweeping across the pine trees before disappearing as the car went into a couple of steep dips in the road. It came out of the last dip, over a rise, and straight for the cabin. I waited for the car to slow; it did and turned into the driveway. I picked up the .38, listening to the car tires crackling on the loose gravel. The car came to a stop in front of the porch, its headlights shining on the window. The room was dark except for an elongated strip of light on the ceiling from the headlights. Pappy killed the lights and got out of the LeBaron. I stepped away from the window, hearing the car door slam shut, and crouched behind the sofa in the pitch-black. I'd let Pappy open the door. I heard him fumbling trying to get the key in the lock on the other side of the door. It was as dark outside as it was inside. The door opened with a jerk, and a .38 came through the door first at the end of an extended arm, followed by Pappy.

"Where are you?" he whispered, groping for the light switch. "Prado, are you here?"

He was still using my name liberally. "I'm here," I said.

"Is that you Prado?"

"If it isn't, you're in a lot of trouble…. Put the gun on the floor and step away from it."

"What for?"

"Guns have a way of going off by accident. Just put it down, Pappy." He put the gun on the floor and pushed it away from him with his foot.

"Where are the lights?"

"Don't turn on the lights," I said. "What's the gun for?"

"I got worried when I saw the place was dark."

"How did everything go?"

"Everything went according to plan."

"Did it?" I was still talking to him from behind the sofa. "No problems?"

"None," he was squinting in the direction of my voice. "Spyro did what he was told. He didn't even bug me about Sheila – Is she sleeping?"

It's Sheila, now, I thought. "I suppose so."

"You know, I think we can pull this off. I walked in and out of that cash room as free as you please."

"Are you alone, Pappy?"

"What do you mean, am I alone?" he asked. "Of course, I'm alone. What do you think…I brought an army with me?"

"I ask you again, Pappy…are you alone?"

"I told you…What do you think – I'm lying? Listen if I'm double crossing you, it'd be easy enough to kill me."

"The light switch is on the left side of the door," I stood up. "It's low on the wall." He flicked on the lights. He was wearing his Phillies shirt and a pair of blue slacks his brother had given him. He looked exhausted. "Pick up your gun before you trip over it, and I'll make you some coffee."

"I'm tired," he was shuffling toward the bedroom.

"You can sleep later," I said. "You can sleep in tomorrow – all morning, but not in there. I'll sleep in there tonight; you sleep in the other bedroom."

"What were you two up to all day?" he smiled wearily. He didn't realize it, but each needling remark he made to me bought him an extra bullet from the cylinder.

"I took your suggestion, and we played cards.... Now let's talk about your day."

I fed him black coffee and crackers, and he told me all about his day – from when he walked into his brother's house until he left the men's room for the second time wearing his fake beard and drove back to the cabin. His brother had given him a crash course on the job and all it entailed, concentrating on what he would be doing and how he would be doing it when they switched places. They'd been together in the house all day up until the time his brother had to leave for the ballpark. His brother had asked about his wife one time, and Pappy told him she was all right and would call him at twelve noon tomorrow. His brother hadn't returned to the subject of his wife again, which I found puzzling considering his attitude last night.

Pappy had left for the ballpark in my car a half an hour after his brother. They were dressed the same except for the fake beard and baseball cap Pappy was wearing. When he arrived at the park, he'd purchased a reserved seat behind home plate and sat in it until the second out was made in the top of the ninth. Then he'd left his seat and gone into the men's rest room next to the club offices. He'd sat in the first stall on the left in a row of five stalls and removed his beard and baseball cap and waited as people filed in and out. Thirteen minutes later by his watch, the door to the stall next to him had opened, and a second later he'd heard four taps on the panel dividing the stalls. He'd passed the beard, cap, watch and sunglasses under the panel to his brother in the next stall and received his brother's I.D. tag, watch, wedding ring and sunglasses. Two minutes later, he'd entered the security code into the outside door to the cash room. The door had opened and closed behind him. He'd stood in the corridor waiting for the guard to visually I.D. him. The guard's face had appeared in the window of the inside door, and then the door had hissed open allowing him to enter the cash room.

"This is important," I asked. "When you came back into the cash room – I mean when you entered the cash room for the first time did the guard scan you?"

"No, he didn't do anything,"

"Did anybody else leave the room while you were there and come back?"

"Let me think," he took a sip of coffee. "Yeh, Mike, the supervisor, left for about ten minutes and came back."

"Did the guard scan him?"

Pappy shook his head in the negative. "Good," I patted him on the shoulder. "Very good, Pappy." I felt generous of heart; I could forgive all human weakness.

"I sat at the middle table," he said, "and just picked up where Spyro had left off. There were different stacks of checks and cash, and he'd been totaling them up, and adding them to different revenue columns on a sheet of paper. I can't be sure, but I might've added some wrong figures to the wrong columns while I was there. If Spyro didn't catch my mistakes, his figures ain't going to jive." He yawned heavily, put his elbows on the table, and rested his head in his hands.

"They're going to have a lot bigger problem to worry about than that tomorrow night." I poured him another cup of coffee. "I agree with you, Pappy. I think we can pull this off."

"I stayed exactly a half hour. That open safe was staring at me the whole time, too. There's a pile of money in that safe – at least there was tonight."

"Did anybody talk to you while you were in there?"

"Everybody was busy. The one woman asked me how my eyes were; I told her they were bothering me a little, and I didn't talk to anybody. I kept my mouth shut."

"What did you tell the guard when you left?"

"Same thing I told the lady," he yawned. "My eyes were bothering me, and I wanted to put some drops in them."

"Is there anybody in there we have to worry about?"

"No, Mike's a tall thin guy in his late fifties, I think. The woman, Evelyn, is about the same age. Gary, the other guy, is younger – late thirties probably, but he couldn't be more than five feet five."

"What about the guard?"

"He's got a .45 on his hip," he said sleepily. "He's in his late twenties I'd say...." His voice trailed off; he could hardly keep his eyes open.

"Go on," I poked him in the arm.

"...I'd say," he roused himself, "if you put a gun in his face, you don't have to worry about him any more than the others." He picked up a cracker, contemplated it, and then closed his eyes. His head nodded forward and the cracker fell out of his hand to the floor.

"You better call it a night, Pappy," I prodded him again. I reached down to pick up the cracker as he got to his feet, and my eyes fell on his shoes – his shoes. "Sonofabitch," I jerked my head up and banged it on the underside of the table. "Did you remember to switch your shoes?"

"My shoes?" he looked down at his brown loafers uncomprehendingly.

"Your shoes! Did you remember to switch shoes with him in the stall?"

I could tell by the look on his face, he hadn't. "I forgot," he said dully. "You never said a word about it; you should've reminded me."

"Goddamn it!"

He was right; I should've reminded him. You were expected to lead the blind. It wasn't the first mistake I'd made on this job, but it might be the last – Stupid sonofabitch that I was, doubly stupid because I expected Pappy to have remembered something I'd forgotten. There were good reasons to change shoes during work, but I couldn't think of any reasons to change back again a half hour later. Maybe, the difference between the shoes wasn't noticeable.

"What kind of shoes did he have on, Pappy?"

"I'm not sure...."

"Were they sneakers, sandals...dress shoes like yours – What?"

"I remember looking at his feet under the stall," he was rubbing his eyes. "I know he had dark socks on like me – Yeh...I remember, he had dress shoes on. They were loafers.... I can't remember the color."

"Never mind," I waved him to bed as you would a contrary child. "Go to bed, Pappy. You need some rest."

He went into the other bedroom and then kept going back and forth to the bathroom before he finally went into the bedroom and stayed there. I checked on the wife to make sure she was asleep. Her face was turned toward the wall, but I listened to her breathing, and it sounded regular. I took a quick shower, shaved, had a cup of coffee, and then lay in the upper bunk and tried to sleep. The room was stuffy as hell, so I opened the window. I listened to her shifting in her sleep on the mattress below me, trying to settle into a comfortable position with her hands cuffed to the headboard. I couldn't sleep thinking about why Pappy's brother had kept his mouth shut about the shoes. He certainly must've noticed with his orderly mind, so why didn't he switch shoes with his brother? Maybe the shoes were so similar he didn't consider it necessary. That was one explanation; I was wondering if there was another one when a sound grabbed my attention: the patter of rain on the cabin roof. I jumped out of the bunk and went to the window. It was pouring outside; the breeze coming through the screen was spraying my chest with a cool mist. The possibility of a rainout had never occurred to me. It hadn't occurred to me to check a weather forecast for the weekend. Since the weather was out of my control, maybe I'd subconsciously dismissed it, not wanting to even think about it, but I was thinking about it now.

I turned on the radio and tried to pick up a weather forecast for close to half an hour before giving up and going back to bed. If it rained it rained; to hell with it, I thought. I needed to get some sleep. If the twin bill was rained out, it would take the job down the drain with it. I had to get some sleep. It felt like everybody in the world was sleeping except me. I lay on my back and listened to the rain drumming on the roof. The rain had brought out the humidity, and it was drawing the sweat out of me. I think it was the humidity; maybe it was just my turn to sweat.

At The End Of The Rainbow

The knock on the door startled me, and I lost my balance, stumbling back against the sink, my pants around my ankles. She wasn't supposed to be home.

"Open the door."

"Wait a second, mother." For some odd reason, my jeans had shrunk; I couldn't pull them up.

"I have to go to the toilet."

"Wait a second."

"Why is this door locked? What are you doing in there?" The doorknob kept turning...turning.

"Leave me alone."

"Is someone in there with you?" The banging on the door was persistent. Why was she home? I wanted to wake up. She'd see.... She was on the other side of the door. Why couldn't I wake up? "I have to go to the bathroom."

I was too susceptible tonight; she was a symbol. "Go away. I can make you go away." It was a dream; I only had to open my eyes to put an end to it.

"I have to go to the bathroom."

It was so annoying I couldn't wake up; I couldn't make this figment go away. "I hear you."

"I have to go to the bathroom."

"I hear you," I woke up. There were no degrees of waking; I was wide awake immediately – no lingering sense-impressions. I opened my eyes and was completely awake. She was banging the bunk bed railing with her foot.

"I have to go to the bathroom."

"I hear you." I went down the ladder and went through the pockets of my pants searching for the key.

"Hurry up." She looked awful, her face haggard and drained of color. Everything about her looked exhausted – except her eyes. Her eyes looked rabid. When I unlocked her cuffs, she scurried for the bathroom. I'd been letting her close the door when she went to the bathroom, and I did this time, too, but this time I heard the lock click. She started screaming at the top of her lungs. I put my shoulder to the door and it splintered open, part of the doorjamb coming with it. She had the window open and was still screaming as she tried to remove the screen. I put my arm around her waist and yanked her away from the window, putting my hand over her mouth. She bit me, so I spun her around and clipped her on the jaw sending her sprawling into the bathtub, taking the shower curtain with her.

I lifted her out of the tub, took her back to the bedroom, and put her in the lower bunk. I put the handcuffs on her again and then put some tape over her mouth. If she still had to go to the bathroom, she could go in the bed. I went outside and stood on the porch. There was no one in sight – certainly no one within shouting distance. It was a gray morning; a light drizzle was falling sideways in a stiff wind.

I went back inside and turned on the radio. I got a weather forecast right off the bat: "...Showers and drizzle this morning, but this whole thing will blow out of here by early afternoon, and the clouds will give way to mostly sunny skies. The high today will be eighty-two, the low sixty-eight. Tomorrow will be sunny and warmer – " I clicked off the radio. At least the weather was cooperating, I thought, as I examined the bite mark on the palm of my hand. I was lucky the skin wasn't broken because there was no antiseptic in the cabin to put on it.

I began a debate with myself on whether or not I should kill her and forego the phone call to the husband. Pappy's bedroom door was still closed. He'd slept through all the commotion. There were risks involved in both courses of action. It came down to considering and then balancing their respective temperaments against the risks. I decided to proceed as planned. I wouldn't kill her now, but her last few hours on earth were not going to be very comfortable.

After I got dressed, I put on some coffee and made jelly toast for breakfast. This was the morning of the night it was going to happen. I sat there munching on toast and wishing it would happen now and not tonight, feeling the sense of anticipation rising in me, knowing I'd be wasting nervous energy all day I should be saving for the job.

Pappy got up at ten o'clock, and when he saw the bathroom door, he swore to himself and came into the kitchen. "What the hell happened?"

"She got a little frisky," I said, pouring him a cup of coffee. "Started yelling...I had to shut her up again – Leave her alone; she'll keep for now until we're ready to make the call."

Pappy went into the bathroom, and I heard the door creaking in protest on its hinges when he tried to close it. I finished my coffee on the front porch. A fine mist was still falling, but the sky was blue above the hills to the west, and there were glimpses of blue behind the caravan of thick gray clouds crawling across the sky. Once in a while the sun would peek out, poking fingers of gold light through the clouds.

By the time I'd finished my second cup of coffee and smoked a cigarette, there were only leftover sprinkles from a few straggling clouds, but the sun was goosing them along, and they were scattering fast. A cloud shaped like a string bean slid across the face of the sun creating a halo effect, and then I saw the rainbow, faint but present, arching from east to west, part of it obscured by the cloud.

"Hey, Pappy," I called into the cabin. He came out bare-chested, his paunch pushing against his belt buckle. "Look at the rainbow, Pappy." He stood on the porch steps in his bare feet, patting his belly, the sun shining full on his unshaven face.

"It looks like it winds up in Redvale," he said. "You know what's at the end of that rainbow? Our pot of gold is at the end of that rainbow."

"Why, Pappy," I said impressed. "I didn't know you were capable of such a beautiful metaphor."

"I'm hungry," he replied and went back inside.

It was a beautiful metaphor, I thought. He just had the possessive pronoun wrong.

*****

I took the car and drove around looking for a phone booth, finally locating one on route 82 in front of a gas station that was out of business. It was about fifteen minutes from the cabin. When I got back to the cabin, I went into the bedroom and Pappy was sitting on the edge of the bed talking to her while he held her feet in his hands and massaged them. She started crying as soon as she saw me. I told Pappy to go put on his beard, sunglasses and cap just to be on the safe side when we went out.

"No need to cry," I told her after he'd left the room. "No one's going to hurt you." I slipped a pair of shoes on her feet and then took off the cuffs. I kept the tape on her mouth. I sent Pappy down to the end of the driveway and waited at the door with her for the all clear sign from him and then walked her to the car. I put her on the floor in the back while Pappy jogged up the driveway. I sat on the passenger side, and he got behind the wheel and started the car. I took the .38 from my pocket, draped my left arm over the seat, and trained the gun on her. "Just behave yourself back there."

"Which way?" Pappy asked.

"Make a right," I said.

As he coasted down the driveway, a park ranger's jeep pulled into it. There was one ranger in the jeep. I put the visor down on my side. I saw the badge and the brown shirt and the trooper hat. I couldn't see his weapon, but I knew he had one. Pappy hit the brakes, and the car skidded. For a split-second, I thought it was going to skid right into the jeep.

"Jesus H. Christ," Pappy said.

"Take it easy; he's alone. Get the hell out and head him off. He's probably just checking on the people staying at the cabins. Tell him we're on our way to meet your wife for lunch in Morgantown – and smile for Christ sake." I looked out the windshield with a smile on my face while I pressed the gun against her ribs. "If you even twitch, I'll kill you," I said to her under my breath.

The ranger took off his hat and placed it on the seat and then got out as Pappy came around to the driver's side of the jeep. Pappy shook his hand.

"I hope you folks are enjoying yourself," the ranger said. He glanced at me and I dropped my eyes pretending I was tuning the car radio. A cop only had to take one good look at my face to know I was trouble.

"Yes, we are," Pappy answered. "It's nice to get away from it all once in a while. My friend and I are on our way to meet my wife in Morgantown for lunch."

"Well, I won't hold you up. I just wanted to remind you to drop off the keys to the cabin at the ranger station when you leave tomorrow. If no one's there, just put them in the slot in the door."

"We will, thanks."

"Enjoy your lunch," the ranger looked up at the sky. "Looks like it's turning into a beautiful day." He got back in the jeep, put his hat on, and then backed out of the driveway and drove off in the direction of the lake. The wife hadn't moved a muscle; she should have. She should've kicked and thrashed and flailed and done everything in her power to attract the attention of the ranger. It was her last chance. She had absolutely nothing to lose except a couple hours of her life, but she still didn't know that – not for sure. Human nature, you see. She still was hanging on to the shred of hope we wouldn't kill her. Human nature – sometimes it came in very handy if you were working on the other side of the law.

When Pappy got back in the car, he was sweating because of the fake beard or the close call or both. "For a second, I thought we were dead."

"Relax," I said. "You heard him."

"I heard him, but I was thinking if he walks up to the car and looks in the back.... Whe-w-w-w." He shivered theatrically and flicked the sweat off the bridge of his nose with his index finger.

"Pappy, you have your hands full worrying about what's going to happen without worrying about what didn't happen."

He put the car in gear and made the right turn onto the road. I directed him to 82 and five minutes later we were pulling into the gas station.

"Park it so the car is between the phone and the road," I told Pappy. It was a few minutes after twelve. Pappy dialed the number while I waited in the car with her. He listened for a moment and then motioned to me. I got out and helped her up from the floor of the car, keeping a vice grip on her arm while walking her over to the phone booth – It wasn't a phone booth, just a phone on a stanchion with a small shelf for the phone book which was long gone, so I wanted to make this as quick as possible because we had no cover on the lot except the car screening us from the road.

We flanked her and Pappy put the phone to her ear. "Tell your husband you're fine," I peeled the tape from her mouth. "No one's hurt you, and no one will hurt you if he continues to cooperate."

"Spiro," she gasped. "It's me – " she hesitated. He was talking. Pappy took the phone from her ear and listened.

"Tell him to shut up and listen," I yelled.

"You heard that," Pappy said. He put the phone back to her ear.

"I'm all right," she said. "I'm fine...listen to me.... They won't hurt me if you do what they say – " I slapped the tape on her mouth and then grabbed the phone from Pappy.

"Four o'clock," I blurted. "We'll be there at four." I hung up the phone. "That as they say is that." She kicked me in the shin and tried to wrench free, but she wasn't going anywhere except to the floor of the car. I sat in the back with her on the return drive to the cabin.

*****

We packed up everything when we got back right down to the orange peels and the cracker crumbs. Then I spent the next two hours wiping the place clean of prints; I went over every square inch of the cabin that some hot shot lab hound might be able to lift a print from. At two thirty I sent Pappy outside to put the bags in the trunk while I went into the bedroom to kill the wife. Her eyes were on me as soon as I entered the room. She was like a cornered animal now, operating purely on instinct – mad with fear, watching every movement of an approaching predator, her blue eyes straining in their sockets. When she saw me take the .38 from my pocket, she froze for a moment and then started squirming and twisting futilely to free herself from the handcuffs, rubbing her face against the bed sheet trying to get the tape off her mouth. I picked up a pillow and she made a low moaning noise under the tape that wanted to rise in volume to a scream but couldn't, so found its release instead as a loud snort from her nose.

"Close your eyes," I told her calmly. My finger was on the trigger and my hand was steady. "Close your eyes," I said. Her eyes were bulging out of their sockets. I felt them burning into the back of my skull. I pressed the pillow against her face and dug the muzzle of the gun into the pillow. I didn't pull the trigger; I couldn't pull the trigger. It came as a complete surprise to me. I thought I could kill her right up to the moment I couldn't kill her. I flung the pillow against the wall disappointedly, put the gun away, and went to plan B. I would be able to kill her when I got my hands on the money. The money was still an abstract concept in my mind; it needed to be a tangible asset sitting in my hands. I needed to see it, touch it, smell it – You better believe a pile of money had a smell to it, like a sunshine scented breeze curling the curtains on the morning of a brand new, never before seen day, full of possibilities – like a present you'd prayed for wrapped in shiny paper under the bough of a Christmas tree. I needed to get my hands on the money; that would provide the proper motivation. I could kill her then; I could kill them all.

She was gagging and choking on her sobs, struggling for breath. I removed the tape from her mouth and she gasped loudly "Plea-s-se don't...d-don't," she sobbed.

"Calm down," I said. "I told you I wasn't going to hurt you.... Stop your crying."

"I d-don't want to die.... I don't –"

"You're not dying. Relax, you're all right."

When I left the bedroom, Pappy was waiting for me. He put his palms up and shrugged his shoulders in a puzzled gesture. "Did you do it?" he asked warily. "I didn't hear a shot."

"It can wait until after we pull the job." I went out on the porch for a cigarette. Pappy followed right behind me.

"But why? I thought you —"

"You thought wrong," I said. "Keep your eye on her until I get back. I mean just your eyes — nothing else, and anything you touch before we leave make sure you wipe clean."

"Where are you going?"

"We need more duct tape."

I found a chain hardware store in Morgantown and bought some more duct tape. The trip took forty minutes. By the time I got back, it was close to three, and we didn't have any time to waste if we wanted to get to the house by four. I wrapped more tape around her arms and mouth, and Pappy put so much tape around her legs she looked like a mummy from the waist down. Then I carried her into the bathroom, put her in the tub, and cuffed her to the faucet in such a way that if she tried to change position she'd dislocate her arms. I stood there looking around the bathroom making sure I wasn't forgetting anything. I looked at the damned faucets ten times before it finally dawned on me what came out of those faucets, and we wouldn't be here to turn them off if she managed to turn on one or both of them. The water would run all day and flood the place and maybe attract attention. I slid open the wooden panel concealing the pipes in the wall between the tub and the toilet and turned off the hot and cold water knobs to the tub.

"That ought to do it," I said. "I suggest you not struggle because the more you do, the more uncomfortable you'll be. You're not going anywhere so just relax. We'll be back tonight."

"When I get back, Sheila," Pappy said, "I'll run some water in that tub and get in with you."

We made sure everything was locked up and secure and then we left.

The plan was, or to put it exactly, the plan Pappy thought we were operating under was to arrive at the house at four o'clock; go over the details one more time with Pappy and his brother; let his brother go to the ballpark at five; wait until the first game is over and then go to the ballpark in my car; park several blocks from the park; separate and walk the rest of the way and buy tickets in different sections of the park; in the top of the seventh, if the Phillies are winning, we go to the men's room, and I change clothing while Pappy waits in the last stall on the left; I slip into the supply room unnoticed, lock it from the inside, and hide behind the bread trays; exactly ten minutes after the last out of the game, Pappy's brother goes to the men's room and switches places with him; he then leaves the ballpark and waits in his car while Pappy enters the cash room; twenty minutes after Pappy enters the cash room, I put in the security code and enter the first door; Pappy opens the second door for me; five minutes later we leave the cash room; we exit by the employee's entrance; Pappy's brother is waiting outside in his car to pick us up; he takes us to my car; we make sure his car is clean and leave it behind, and Pappy drives all of us back to the cabin in my car. Here's where my plan and the plan Pappy thinks we're operating under diverge. It was a diversion with major ramifications for Pappy.

*****

I dropped him off in the alleyway behind the house, and he went inside while I parked the car. When I came in they were sitting side-by-side on the sofa, dressed in the same blue slacks and Phillies shirts, except Pappy had brown loafers and his brother had black.

"Were you wearing those shoes last night?" I asked him as soon as I was inside the kitchen door.

"Yes."

"I already told him about it," Pappy said.

"You remembered everything else. Why did you forget that?"

"I just forgot. I had a lot on my mind."

"Do you have another pair of black loafers for your brother to wear tonight?"

"No, this is the only pair I have."

"Well, don't forget to switch shoes tonight. Don't forget one thing tonight or you won't be around to remember anything tomorrow."

"Don't worry," Pappy said. "Spiro won't forget anything."

"Who are you, his spokesperson?" I snapped at Pappy. "Let Spiro tell me."

"I was just saying, you don't have to worry," Pappy assured me. "We won't forget anything."

They looked at each other and then they looked at me. I stared first at one and then the other. They were twins, so I didn't care how goddamned long they'd been apart. Each could probably tell what the other was thinking, but I couldn't tell what they were thinking. I leveled my stare at Pappy's brother. "I've been here five minutes, and you haven't asked me about your wife – Why?"

"He asked me about her," Pappy chimed in again. "I told him as long as he cooperated she wouldn't be hurt."

"But he didn't ask me about her," I said. "That's the difference."

"You'd just tell me what I want to hear...just like my brother," Spiro said. "What would be the point?"

"The point would be that you're asking about her because she's your wife and you're worried about her." His attitude was bothering me. I could tell it was different as soon as I stepped in the door. Where before, he was agitated and submissive, now he seemed collected and in control. Maybe over the past forty-eight hours he'd simply come to the conclusion the best chance for his wife and him to walk away in one piece was to do what he was told. Maybe his attitude was one of resignation and no more. Maybe I was just walking off the nervous energy that had been building in me all day, and it was all in my imagination, but I could've sworn I saw a look in his eye when he glanced at Pappy exactly like the look Ely Lovelock had in his eye after he'd palmed those dice – He knew something the house didn't.

"We have fifty minutes," I told him, looking at my watch, "before you have to leave for the ballpark, and we're going to go back over every detail just be sure everything is clear in our minds. I don't want any mistakes tonight; I don't want anybody forgetting to switch shoes or anything else. I saw a pot of coffee on the stove when I came in – bring it in and hurry the hell up."

I waited for him to leave the room, and then I sat down next to Pappy, took the .38 out of my pocket, and rested it on my knee. "It's dangerous to get in my way when I'm so close to getting my hands on what I want."

"What are you talking about?" he frowned.

"Just that it's dangerous to make me nervous," I held the gun in front of his face. "Seeing the two of you together makes me very nervous."

"I don't know what you're talking about," he insisted. He was looking straight at me. I'll give him that; he didn't drop his eyes. His one eye was framed by the trigger guard on the .38. "Honest to God."

I put the .38 back in my pocket. "It's a little late in the day to be working up some real family feeling.... Do you know what I mean?"

"Hell, you don't have to worry," he whispered. "I'm just doing what you told me; I'm trying to get along with him, so he won't blow up at me and screw up the job. I'm just being friendly, you know, but nothing's changed. Nothing has changed."

"No change of heart?"

"Me...are you kidding?"

"Just remember that pot of gold at the end of the rainbow, Pappy."

"When the time comes, I won't blink an eye."

Either will I, I thought.

The Heist

Pappy's brother left at quarter to five for the ballpark, but not before I had to remind him to put on his sunglasses. We listened to the first game on the radio; it was a pitcher's duel with two quick workers on the mound and flew by in two hours – the Phillies losing two to one. After we wiped everything we'd handled, we left for the game in my car. I parked four blocks away on Amity Street, and then we walked separately to the park.

I heard the public address announcer going over the starting line ups for the second game as I walked across Front Street to the turnstiles. I bought a general admission ticket in the left field corner; we had agreed I would sit down the left field line, and Pappy would sit down the right field line. The place was packed with fans. For the first four innings, I sat in the left field deck bar nursing a beer at a wrought iron table with the Phillies carryall on my lap. Then I found a grandstand seat behind the visitor's bullpen. The nightcap dragged like hell. There were a lot of pitching changes, and each reliever worked slower than the guy he'd replaced.

In the top of the sixth, Altoona broke the game open with a five spot, thinning out the disgruntled crowd considerably. A sweep by Altoona meant the Phillies would be out of the play-offs. It was shaping up as a bad day for the Redvale Phillies baseball club. By the bottom of the seventh, the score was thirteen to six, and most of what was once a capacity crowd were in their cars headed home. I went down the ramp, walked behind the grandstands and the picnic area, through the concourse and into the men's room. The place was jammed with people, and all of the stalls were taken. Pappy was waiting at the first stall on the left; he didn't look at me.

"Stupid bastards," I said to myself. They can't wait until they get home to take a crap; they'd rather take one on a filthy toilet in a public restroom. The last stall door on the left opened, and a fat kid waddled out, and Pappy went in. I had to wait five minutes for another stall to open before I could change my clothing. I took off my shirt, stuffed it in my carryall, and put on the Phillies shirt and then the apron and hat and a pair of latex gloves. I pinned the courtesy badge Pappy's brother had given me to the apron. By the time I left the men's room, there were two outs in the bottom of the seventh. I watched the last out on closed circuit TV by the Phillies clubhouse. I checked my watch; it was 10:40.

There were two supply rooms for the concessions across from the cash room and offices on the other side of the turnstiles. I waited with my back to the wall next to one of the open supply doors for a knot of fans headed for the exits to shield me and then slipped into the supply room, locking the door behind me. Stacks of red and blue bread trays, some full and some empty, took up most of the space in the room. A single bare bulb hung from the ceiling. I found a hiding place between a stack of trays and the wall opposite the door. All I could do now was wait for 11:15. My heart was pounding in my chest as I leaned against the cement wall. I was actually trembling with anticipation.

At 11:05, I heard somebody trying the door. He stopped, and there were a few moments of silence. Then I heard a key going in the lock, and I scrambled from behind the trays, picking up one filled with hot dog rolls as the door opened. A guy came in dressed in a green work uniform pulling a hand truck in the door after him. He was wearing a yellow baseball cap with Meyer's Bakery sewn in script on it. He stopped dead in his tracks when he saw me standing there.

"Didn't you hear me out there?" he asked. He didn't wait for my answer. "Why did you lock the door?"

"I didn't realize it locked behind me." He was staring at me, his eyes narrowed. He didn't know what was going on, but he was wondering. In any case, he'd remember my face. I kicked the door closed with my foot and then held out my arms and let the tray drop. He watched it hit the floor, and in the next second I had the .38 in my hand. I swung hard and caught him high on the forehead with the butt of the gun and the blood spurted. He grunted, staggering back against the hand truck, and fell to his knees. I swung again and hit him just above the ear, and he went over on his side. His one leg was twitching, so I hit him again, same spot, and his leg stopped twitching. He was bleeding like hell from the gashes in his head, the blood spreading in a pool on the floor. I grabbed him by the ankles and hauled him out of sight behind the stacks of trays. He left a trail of blood behind him. It was 11:08 – seven more minutes. I looked at the guy stretched out on his stomach. I didn't know if he was dead or alive, and I didn't care because either way he wasn't going to be remembering my face. Bad timing on his part, I thought as I watched the blood inching across the cement floor toward my feet. Bad timing, pure and simple – nothing more and nothing less. One minute out of a billion minutes in his life, but during that one minute he got in my way. The blood was still pouring out of him, so I tore open a few bread loaves and scattered the slices of bread on the floor to sop up the blood.

At 11:15, I opened the door a crack and looked out. There was no one at the exits. I stepped out and closed the door. I was holding a bread tray in one hand and the carryall in the other. There were several guys in yellow shirts at the far end of the concourse on the right field side and a few workers still cleaning up behind the counters of their concession stands. I walked casually over to the cash room door, keeping my head down, took the mask out of the bag, punched in the security code, and opened the door; walking through, the door swung shut behind me as I put on the mask. I was locked in the corridor, and I didn't see Pappy's face in the window of the inside door. I stayed right where I was, afraid to move. If something had gone wrong, I was a rat in a trap. I'd still be standing here when the cops arrived. My face was burning under the mask, the blood pounding in my temples. I heard somebody on other side of the door yell; it sounded like Pappy, but I couldn't be sure. Somebody yelled again, and Pappy's face appeared in the window. I heard a loud click and a hissing noise, and then the door opened slowly on its big hinges. I entered the cash room, my heightened sense of awareness making my spine tingle, taking in everything immediately; the guard lying face down on the floor with his hands clasped behind his neck; two other employees, Mutt and Jeff types, lying in the same position between the counting tables; a woman in a chair crying, her shoulders shaking, the tears rolling down her cheeks and spotting her pink slacks; the stacks of cash and checks on the counting tables; the doors of the black floor safe wide open; Pappy in a fevered state sweating through his Phillies shirt – He was holding his piece in one hand and a .45 in the other; I took the .45 from him and held it on the guard.

"Tape up that big sonofabitch," I handed him a roll of duct tape from the carryall. "He might get restless." My voice sounded different under the mask. I addressed the others, "We'll be out of here in two minutes; in the meantime, keep your mouths shut and don't move. If you move, I'll shoot you – simple as that." The woman clamped both hands over her mouth and bent forward in the chair.

When Pappy finished duct-taping the guard, I tucked the .45 under my apron and started sliding the stacks of cash from the tables into the open carryall. "Keep your gun on them," I told Pappy. I cleaned off the tables and then moved to the safe. My eyes got wide when I saw all the packs of twenties and fifties. I emptied the safe except for the coin.

"Did I get it all?" I asked Pappy.

"There's a box on the floor by the door –"

I stepped over the guard who was lying on his side and walked over to the metal box on the floor. There were a half dozen bank bags in it. I was jamming the bags in the carryall which was now stuffed full when a red light on the door started flashing and a buzzer went off.

"Someone's coming in," Pappy said.

"Is it an employee?" Pappy nodded. "Open the door – hurry up." I flattened myself against the wall as he pulled down a red lever set in the door. The door opened with a hiss. A white-haired guy with knobby knees wearing one of those yellow shirts and plaid shorts took a step in the door and stopped when he saw the guard on the floor. I grabbed him by the shirtfront and pulled him in the rest of the way.

"What's going on here?" he asked feebly.

"Shut up and get over there," I took the walkie-talkie from his belt.

He looked at Pappy for further clarification. "Spiro, what are you doing? Are you crazy? You can't get away with this. You –"

"I said shut up," I poked him in the back of the neck with the muzzle of the .38. "Move, get in the back – all of you in the back. Come on, goddammit – move. Keep an eye on this one on the floor, Spiro." The others got up from the floor, and I herded them into a utility closet behind the safe. The tall guy was supporting the woman who was letting out drawn out sobs and then gasping for air. I packed them in shoulder to shoulder in the closet. "I wouldn't be in too much of a hurry to get out of there," I told them. "I might just be waiting out here to shoot the first one that comes through the door." When I closed the door, the woman let out a little shriek that sounded like a hiccup. I locked the door and wedged a chair under the doorknob. I looked at my watch; three minutes had passed since I'd punched in the security code.

"Did you remember not to touch anything in here?" I asked Pappy.

"I didn't touch anything except the door lever and the stuff sitting on that middle table – the stack of checks and the pencil and spread sheet."

I crammed all of it in the carryall and then wiped the door lever clean of prints with my handkerchief.

"I just thought of something," Pappy grabbed my arm and whispered. "The way these doors work – how are we getting out of here, Prado?"

I backhanded him across the face, and he recoiled. "You dumb sonofa..." I said. I looked down at the guard; he was looking at me, his eyes wide and bright with fear. He knew I knew he'd heard, and he also knew I had to do something about it. I couldn't shoot him – too noisy, so I looked around the room for a quiet way to do it. My eyes fell on a metal paperweight in the shape of a miniature bat on top of a stack of papers on the guard's desk. When the guard saw me pick it up, he tried to squirm away from me. I turned him over on his back, his hands taped under him, and when I put my knees on his chest, Pappy turned away. The guard made a shrill whine under his taped mouth that sounded like a dentist's drill before I hit him on top of the head, and then his eyes rolled up and his body stiffened. I hit him again and his body relaxed. I hit him one more time, and I felt his skull crack. I stood up and threw the bloody paperweight on the desk. "Look at what you did to him," I told Pappy. "Because of your stupidity, this guy ain't going home."

"Let's get the hell out of here," Pappy said weakly, keeping his back turned to me.

"Yeh, you've made me waste enough time." I zipped up the carryall and put it under my arm. "Listen...one of us opens this door and lets the other one into the corridor, and then opens the door to the concourse. The door re-locks and then the other guy opens this door again and goes into the corridor. The guy on the outside punches in the security code and opens that door for the guy in the corridor – simple enough."

"Do you want to let me out first?"

"Sure." That was the smart way to do it; the less time I was in the concourse the better. I wasn't worried about Pappy leaving me in the corridor because the money would be with me in the corridor. "How do I work this lever?"

"Just pull down on the red lever until it stops and then let it go. When the door closes, press the black button above the lever. That opens the outside door."

"I pulled down the lever and released it. "Go." Pappy went into the corridor, and I waited for the door to close and then hit the black button. Pappy grabbed the doorknob and went out. I repeated the procedure to get me into the corridor and then waited for the door to close and Pappy to put in the security code. Ten seconds after the inside door had closed, the outside door opened. I took my mask off and slipped into the concourse and wiped the knob with my apron as I had the other doorknobs Pappy had touched. Another guy in a green uniform from Meyer's bakery was banging on the locked supply room door while one of the Ballpark Ambassadors stood by with his walkie-talkie to his ear. Directly across from us a beefy-armed woman with a white hair net covering her bleached-blond hair was glancing at them as she replaced an empty plastic mustard jar on the table in front of a hot dog stand with a full one. When I came out the door, she glanced over at us as we ducked around the corner of the offices into the corridor leading to the employee entrance.

"Spiro," she called. "Hey, Spiro!"

I bucked open the glass double doors and we were outside next to the veteran's monument. Above us, the stadium lights were still on, flooding the night sky inside the brick walls of the park. Car lights blinked off and on down the street. I had my hand under my apron waiting for somebody to come through the double doors after us, but nobody did; I looked around and there wasn't a cop in sight. The car pulled up to the curb in front of us, and Pappy got in the passenger side and took off his sunglasses. His brother was still wearing the beard and baseball cap. I got in the back and put the carryall in my lap. I twisted around and took the .45 from under my belt.

"Make a left on Front," I told him as he pulled away.

"How much do you think we got?" Pappy asked over his shoulder.

"I don't know. We'll have plenty of time to count it later."

"There was a shit load of money in that safe tonight."

I knew exactly how Pappy felt. I hefted the carryall in my lap; it was stuffed with money – my money. I put the bag back on my lap and patted it lovingly like a father patting his child on the head. I wanted to count the money in the bag down to the last dollar; I wanted to count it slowly and savor it. I wanted to put the denominations in separate stacks and watch the stacks rise higher as I counted toward an end total I could only guess would be as beautiful as the end of that rainbow poor Pappy had talked about, but the counting would have to wait until the job was done. They weren't expecting a heist despite all their precautions to the contrary. It was the last thing they were expecting; they were casual and careless. It had been as easy as walking into a drugstore, getting a prescription filled, and walking out. It only remained for me to tie up a few loose ends. I would have to kill Pappy, his brother and the wife, and then the circle would be complete – no witnesses left alive to point a positive finger at me, no evidence. I would be an unidentified accomplice. It was perfect as a circle. The three of them would be inside the circle under a ton of evidence, and I would be infinitely outside the circle with only the money to connect me to the crime – my money.

I rolled down the window to listen for sirens. "Make another left at Amity and go to the end of the block."

"Can I see my wife now?" Spiro asked.

"Just as soon as we get to where we're going."

"I did exactly what you told me; are you going to let us go?"

"I said I would, didn't I? All right, pull in right behind the LeBaron."

He parked the car and we all got out. "We're taking the LeBaron," I informed them. "You're driving, Pappy; put your brother in the back and keep your gun on him." I wiped down his brother's car – steering wheel, interior and exterior door handles. As I was getting into the front seat of the car, I heard the first sirens. I handed Pappy the keys. "We're taking the long way around. Make a u-turn and go back to Front and turn left. We're going to avoid any major roads.

When Pappy made the left, we saw a police car, its siren wailing, coming in the opposite direction. It whizzed past us on the way to the ballpark. A minute later, another police car zoomed past in the same direction. "When you get to the end of Front, take the bridge into West Redvale."

I'd already mapped out the route back to the cabin, and now I directed Pappy through the outlying suburbs – West Redvale, Wessing, Pennington, Grille – When we reached 724, I turned on the radio and tuned it to the local news station. There wasn't a word about the heist at the ballpark. Twenty minutes later we reached Grigsboro. Route 345 which ran through Pierre Creek State Park connected with 724 on the other side of town. About the same time Pappy was making a left onto 345, the local news was coming on at the bottom of the hour. "The story topping WEEV edition of local news is a robbery at United Energy Stadium that left one man dead and another man fighting for his life.... Police authorities report the robbery occurred shortly after the conclusion of the doubleheader at the stadium and involved an employee of the Redvale Phillies and at least one other man. The robbery took place in the cash office where the employee, identified as Spyridon Papademetriou, allegedly allowed another man wearing a mask to gain access to the office. The other man has not been identified. A security guard, Robert Stuber, age twenty-six, of Redvale was killed during the robbery and another man, Marvin Glimp, age forty-nine, of Pennington, an employee of Meyer's Bakery, was beaten and suffered severe head injuries –"

"You killed Bobby," came from the back seat.

"Nobody was supposed to get hurt," I said. "You can blame that on your brother, here."

"I didn't kill anybody," Pappy said.

"Shut up – both of you."

"I didn't think anybody else would be hurt," Pappy's brother slumped back in the car seat. "He had two little boys – and that other man from the bakery –"

"Shut the hell up," I said.

"...He is undergoing surgery at Redvale Hospital at this hour. Based on witness accounts, there might have been a third person involved, a man or woman who drove the getaway car (perfect, I thought). Papademetriou, an employee of the club for six years, is thirty-seven years old and lives in Redvale. Police have put out an all-points bulletin for his car, a white Honda Accord sedan... license plate number GAZ8514. Paul Goldberg, President of the Redvale Phillies, issued this statement: 'I would first like to extend my deepest condolences and the condolences of the ball club to the family and friends of Bob Stuber. He was a fine young man who died in the performance of his duties. His death is tragic and shocking, and I and everyone associated with the Phillies will do everything in our power to help the police apprehend the people responsible for this terrible crime. Our hearts also go out to the family of Mr. Glimp, and we wish him a full recovery. Again, we'll be doing everything possible to assist the police in the capture of these criminals. This is a very sad day for the entire organization.' The WEEV Sunday morning news team with John Courtney will be providing expanded coverage of the robbery with eyewitness accounts from the stadium. Also a – " I switched off the radio.

"Sounds like your good name has been sullied," I said to Pappy's brother. He didn't look at me; he was staring blankly out the car window at the dark wall of woods whizzing by. A corner of his beard was peeling loose. "I wouldn't worry about it too much." He mumbled something under his breath I didn't catch except for one word – Sheila.

The woods cramping the road on the driver's side fell away, and I knew we were passing the lake. I couldn't see it; the moon was down, and there was no reflection of light on the water, only a pitch-black expanse with no dimension. Everything was blackness except for the road ahead under the clearly defined sweep of the headlights. The black cloak of woods swept in tight to the road again, and I knew we were near the cabin, and I thought Pappy knew, but apparently he didn't because he kept driving until I knew he'd driven too far.

"Where the hell are you going? You went past the cabin."

"I was waiting for you to tell me where to turn."

"I wasn't paying attention; I thought you knew where you were going."

Pappy had to maneuver the car back and forth to turn around because the road was narrow and the trees were tight to the road on both sides. "It's so goddamned dark, you can't see a thing," he said as he tugged on the steering wheel. "They should have street lights out here."

"Street lights in the woods," I said impatiently, keeping an eye on his brother in the back. "Enough of your stupidity...just turn the car around and get us back to the cabin. Unless, you'd rather park it here and wait for the sun to come up."

"Take it easy, I don't want to go off the road and end up blowing a tire."

He finally got the car turned around. The rear tires kicked up gravel as he jammed down the gas pedal. "Slow down," I told him. "The driveway is on my side; I'll let you know when it's coming up." We hit a big dip in the road, and I knew the cabin was just ahead. "Slow down...see it?"

"I see it." He pulled into the driveway and I saw the welcoming glow in the cabin window from the one light I'd left on. It was good to be home. Pappy parked the car parallel to the porch and we got out of the car. His brother was still sitting in the back; he hadn't made a move to open the car door.

I ducked my head back in the car, "You stay put until I tell you otherwise." Pappy was on the driver's side; I talked to him over the car roof. "Bring him in afterwards." I pointed my index finger at him and my thumb was the hammer of a gun. He nodded once, and I saw the relief soften his features. He knew what I was going to do, and he didn't want to be there when I did it, just like he didn't want to be there when I shot his brother. He didn't have the stomach for the killing, but he'd be more than happy to grab half the take from the job and slither back to where he came from on that stomach of his. There was one killing he'd have to witness – his own; that was one killing he wasn't going to get out of watching. Poor, stupid Pappy, he thought his hands somehow were clean. Christ, they were dirtier than mine.

I unlocked the cabin door and went inside to kill the wife.

The Evil Twin

I felt for the light switch inside the bathroom door and heard her shift violently in the tub. When I turned on the light, she squinted at me, her eyes not used to the brightness. Disappointment registered in her eyes when she saw it was me and not somebody riding in to the rescue, followed for a split-second by a trace of bewilderment over why I was wearing an apron. Then the dread poured out of her eyes; it could've filled ten bathtubs. It was the dread of the moment. I set the carryall on the toilet seat, put the .45 on top of it, and reached in my pocket for the .38. I'd forgotten something; I went into the bedroom. When she saw me come back with a pillow, she jerked spasmodically in the tub and tried to wrench her hands free of the faucet, but all she succeeded in doing was cutting the skin around her cuffed wrists.

"I'm sorry," I said. "But there's been a change of plans." I kept my eyes off her face; I was too smart for her. I knew I'd see a dying ember of hope in those washed out blue eyes for a last second reprieve. I bent over the tub, covered her face and chest with the pillow, and took the .38 out of my pocket. Then I heard a loud noise. It came from outside the cabin, and it seemed I was sprinting for the door before the nerve in my inner ear had even transmitted the message to my brain that it was a gunshot. I flattened myself against the wall, expecting to see police cars and the usual assemblage that went with them when I peered out the window, but all I saw was my car. Pappy and his brother were nowhere in sight. I cracked open the door, my finger on the trigger of the .38, and called out through the screen. "Pappy, where are you? Pappy...are you all right? Where are you? Pap-p-e-e-e –!"

"I'm back here!" his voice came from somewhere behind the cabin.

"What was that shot?" I wasn't about to venture outside the cabin. "Where's your brother?"

"I shot him!" he cried. "I shot my brother."

When I heard that, I came out on the porch and crept to the corner of the cabin. In the faint glow from the cabin windows, I saw Pappy wading through the knee-high undergrowth at the edge of the woods. When he was clear of the woods, he dropped to his knees, let his .38 fall to the grass, and broke into sobs.

"Where is he?" I asked, running up to him. He didn't answer me, so I knelt beside him, and he put his head in his hands, his brother's I.D. tag dangling from his neck. "Where's your brother?"

"He's...back there...in the woods...." he was choking on his tears.

"Is he dead?"

That set him off. "Yes-s-s-s, he's dead!" he sobbed. "Are you happy now that I saved you the trouble? He's dead – dead. I killed my brother...." I noticed the wedding ring on his finger, and made a mental note to remove it later.

"We have to make sure," I stood up.

"You make sure."

"It's pitch dark in there. You'll have to show me where he is – come on." I helped him to his feet, and he wiped his eyes with the back of his hands. He bent over, picked up his .38, and then I followed him into the woods.

"He make a break for it?" I asked as we stumbled through the undergrowth.

"He just jumped out of the back seat and started running," Pappy sighed. "I told him to stop – I told him I'd shoot – He just kept running into the woods. I had to shoot him...." His voice trailed off.

"You had no choice," I said, mustering up a consoling tone of voice. "You had to do it; otherwise, we'd be two chickens in a pot right now."

We found his brother about twenty yards in. He was on his knees between the roots of a big evergreen tree, slumped against the trunk, his beard half off. It was so goddamned dark, I couldn't tell where he'd been hit. I pulled him on his side, and when my hand went between his shoulder blades, it came away sticky with blood. I wiped my hand on the pine needles. Pappy turned away and broke into a fresh round of sobs, his shoulders shaking.

"We can't just leave him here," Pappy said with his back to me.

"Let's go," I said, pushing him ahead of me. "We have to get back to the cabin; his wife is still in the tub."

"But we can't –"

"Don't worry. The cops will find him when they do a perimeter search."

When we got back to the cabin, Pappy sat on the porch steps and let his head hang. Just one ahead of you, Pappy, I thought as I went back inside the cabin.

The wife had somehow managed to get her legs out of the bathtub apparently in an attempt to reach the .45 on the toilet seat. The only thing she'd succeeded in doing was dislocating one or both of her shoulders. She was moaning heavily, still flopped over the lip of the tub.

"You just make it harder on yourself," I said hoisting her back into the tub as she whimpered in pain. "It hurts like hell, huh? Well..." I picked up my trusty pillow from the floor. When I straightened up, she was looking past me toward the doorway, nodding her head urgently, and the oddest thing was her eyes were wide, not from terror, but from anticipation.

Before I could turn, a gun roared and I felt the heat from the muzzle flame on the back of my neck. I fell against the tub, on my knees, hunched over trying to make myself smaller, trying to get the .38 out of my pocket. The gun roared again, and then I knew what she already knew; I wasn't the target. I looked over the lip of the tub at her. She'd sagged down and the look of anticipation had been frozen out of her dead eyes, and two dark spots that weren't on her blouse before were there now and rapidly increasing in diameter. A gray-blue acrid haze hung in the air like the atmospherics of a nightmare as I continued to try to get the .38

which seemed to have gotten bigger out of my pocket which seemed to have gotten smaller.

"I had to do it myself," a voice whispered behind me – Pappy's voice. "It was the only right thing I could do in this mess."

I turned, still on my knees, and saw the shoes first. I would've noticed the eyes first, but I was on the floor and saw the shoes first – brown shoes. He was wearing brown shoes. Had he forgotten to switch shoes again? He'd remembered everything else; could it be he'd forgotten to switch shoes again? I already knew the answer to that question as I finally got the .38 out of my pocket. God no, I thought, and it was the last conscious thought I ever had. The .38 roared once again before I could lift my own gun, and it felt like a sledge hammer hit me square in the chest. I went to the floor, but the floor did not stop me; it opened up, and I fell into a black hole, black as those woods where I was going to bury Pappy, black as the heart of his brother who'd double-crossed the double-crosser, black as the night. The wind was screaming in my ears as I flailed my arms trying to grab on to something to stop my fall, and then I saw a hand – a woman's hand – like alabaster, slender, with long delicate fingers, and I reached for it, but it was too weak to hold me, far too weak, and I kept falling. I heard another shot; it sounded far away and I felt nothing this time – nothing except a cessation of the wind. I was falling now as if in a vacuum. I was a shell, an integument, a residue of myself; I was weightless – floating but still falling... down...down...down into blackness. Then I knew I'd never see a penny of that money – my money. Because I was dead. I was dead because this hole had no bottom....

Dénouement

A patrol car from the Columbiana Police Department and an unmarked police car from the Detective's Division of the Redvale Police Department pulled up in front of the rundown frame house at 221 Sycamore Road. Two uniformed officers got out of the patrol car, and two men in dark suits and one man in a gray state police uniform got out of the other car and went up the uneven brick walk to the house, the two officers leading the way. When they went up the front steps, they were careful to avoid the middle one which was missing. One of the officers pulled open the squealing screen door and knocked once on the leaded glass pane and only once before the door opened immediately. No surprise or fear registered on the man's face when he saw the five men standing at his door.

"Is your name Stratton Papademetriou?" one of the men dressed in a dark suit asked him.

"Yes," he hesitated ever so slightly.

"This is Detective Slivka" the same man said, "and I'm Lieutenant Cransavage; we're from the Redvale Police Department. These two officers are with the Columbiana Police Department, and this other gentleman is Captain Crawford from the State Police Barracks. May we come in?"

He didn't ask why; he just stepped aside and let them come in, and then led them into the front parlor. The five men stood in a semi-circle facing him.

"Do you have any weapons on you, Mr. Papademetriou?" Captain Crawford asked.

"Of course not," he smiled quizzically.

"Do you mind if we pat you down? It'll only take a moment – Call it a matter of form."

"Help yourself," he lifted his arms and one of the uniformed officers frisked him fast and thoroughly from his shoulders down to his ankles and then nodded at Captain Crawford.

"Do you have identification on you?" Lieutenant Cransavage asked. "May we see it, please?" Papademetriou took his wallet out of his back pocket, took out an Ohio driver's license and handed it to the detective who looked at it and then at him. They all were looking at him with the same cold, accusatory stare policemen could affect without even trying. "Have a seat, Mr. Papademetriou." He sat down in a rosewood armchair with faded upholstery, and the five men regrouped around him.

"Take off your left shoe and sock, please," Detective Slivka told him.

"What – Why should I do that?"

"Just do it," Lieutenant Cransavage said grimly.

"I don't understand this.... You come barging in here treating me like a criminal – not even telling me what it's all about. Don't you need a warrant or something?"

"You mean one of these?" Lieutenant Cransavage took a folded piece of ivory-colored paper out of the inside pocket of his suit coat and held it in front of Papademetriou's face. "Would you like to look at it?" He gave him the warrant and Papademetriou barely glanced at it before handing it back. "Now why don't you save yourself a lot of trouble and take off your shoe and sock?"

He untied his left shoe, took it off, and pulled off his sock. All the men bent over in unison peering at his foot; then they straightened up and Lieutenant Cransavage stepped forward. "Spyridon G. Papademetriou...you are under arrest for the murders of your wife Sheila H. Papademetriou; your brother, Stratton P. Papademetriou and Malcolm Prado –"

"I didn't think you'd check his prints," Papademetriou shrugged, slipping his sock on, and wiggled his foot back into the shoe. One of the officers took his arm, pulled him to his feet, and cuffed his hands behind his back while the other officer read him his rights.

"...You have a right to an attorney; if you cannot afford an attorney, one will be appointed for you by the court.... Do you understand your rights? Sir...do you understand your rights?"

"Yes...yes I understand, but I want to confess."

"You understand," Lieutenant Cransavage said, "you don't have to talk to us without the presence of an attorney – Do you have an attorney, Mr. Papademetriou?"

"I don't want an attorney," he sighed. "I just want to tell you what happened. Who do I talk to? Do I talk to you? What's your name again?"

"Lieutenant Cransavage. You'll have plenty of time to talk. The officers are going to take you down to the station."

"I want to confess."

"So we can expect your cooperation in extradition proceedings?" Captain Crawford asked.

"Why wouldn't I?"

"Do you need anything before we go?" Lieutenant Cransavage asked.

"No...I don't think so, but I would like to lock the place up before we go."

"One of the officers will secure your home for you. Where are your keys?"

"On the kitchen table." Lieutenant Cransavage nodded at one of the officers, and he left the room.

While they waited for the officer to return, Papademetriou sat down again with his hands cuffed behind him and leaned forward in the chair staring down at his foot. "One question," he said. "Why did you want to see my left foot?"

"Just confirming what we already knew," Lieutenant Cransavage said, exchanging a glance with Detective Slivka. "You mentioned about taking his fingerprints – We wouldn't have, of course; there would've been no reason to. The ball club had a set of your prints from the bonding agency in your file, and all evidence at the crime scene and the cabin pointed to you being a victim whose wife was abducted to force your cooperation, and then you both were killed to eliminate any witnesses, and Malcolm Prado was double-crossed by his accomplice who took off with the money."

"I haven't touched a penny of the money," Papademetriou offered. "It's in a safe deposit box at the 6th Street branch of the Columbiana National Bank under my brother's name."

Detective Slivka took a memo pad from his pocket and jotted down the name and location of the bank. "We'll need a bank subpoena," he said as an aside.

"Even if you and your wife were accomplices," Lieutenant Cransavage went on, "the same scenario would have applied in the end. The only prints we lifted at the crime scene belonged to you or the other employees. Somebody knew how to cover their tracks. The only prints we found in your house or your cars belonged to you and your wife – same with the cabin, except for a partial palm print we lifted from your wallet that the FBI wasn't able to identify. There were no other prints, not a shred or scrap of evidence, not a cigarette butt – nothing. So...as I've said, there would've been no reason to take prints from the body."

"But you found a reason, didn't you?"

"Your autopsy gave us a reason," he smiled to himself. "Or should I say, the autopsy on your brother's body gave us a reason. The county coroner performed the autopsies on your brother and your wife – I believe you know the man."

"Yes...Bernie Bischof."

"And you're both members of the Wildenschire Swimming Pool."

"What does that have to do with anything?"

"It seems during the course of the autopsy on what he thought was your body, Dr. Bischof noticed you were missing half of the little toe on your left foot. He couldn't understand this because it was an old injury, and he'd seen you at the pool not more than two weeks before, and you had all ten of your toes then."

Spyridon Papademetriou could only bow his head in the face of this revelation. "There can only be one explanation," he said in a hollow tone.

"Yes sir, there can only be one explanation. The guy lying on the autopsy table with a bullet in his heart was your twin brother. No one knew you had a brother, let alone a twin brother. Apparently, you told everyone you were an only child."

"My wife knows – I mean…she knew."

"We ran his prints through the system," said Lieutenant Cransavage, "and they came up belonging to one Stratton Papademetriou, last address, 221 Sycamore Road, Columbiana, Ohio. It turns out he lost part of his little toe in a machine shop accident in prison four years ago. From there, it was just a matter of putting two and two together. Your brother filled in for you on the autopsy table, so why wouldn't you fill in for him. It made perfect sense."

"So here you are," Papademetriou stood up.

"Here we are," said Lieutenant Cransavage. "But if the coroner hadn't noticed that little toe, your brother would be in the ground now, and you'd be sitting pretty here with – How much was it, Pete?"

"Close to $185,000," Detective Slivka answered.

"…With $185,000 in a safe deposit box."

"Looks like you got tripped up by a little toe," Detective Slivka cracked. Lieutenant Cransavage gave him a disapproving look and took Papademetriou by the arm as the officer came back into the room. He walked him out to the patrol car, put him in the back seat, and then the detective got behind the wheel of his car and followed the cruiser to the Columbiana Police Station.

An officer at the station fingerprinted Papademetriou and took his mug shot. After he processed, he was put in a holding cell in the basement of the station where he spent the night. The next day he was provided counsel and taken before a Common Pleas Judge. During a brief hearing, he waived extradition and was ordered by the judge to be returned to Pennsylvania for trial. He was then transferred to the county prison where he spent the night in an isolation cell. The following morning he was released into the custody of Detectives Cransavage and Slivka who drove him back to Redvale where he was held in Barnes County Prison until his arraignment before Barnes County Judge Bradley Webster who denied bail and ordered him remanded to the county prison.

*****

Dave Hinrichs

Two deputies from the Sheriff's Department escorted their shackled prisoner who was wearing an orange jumpsuit up three, wide stone steps, through heavy glass doors, into a cool, waxed-linoleum hallway. Ahead, to the right was a receiving desk behind a polished banister. Captain Jones was sitting on the banister waiting for the three men. The man standing next to him in a tight brown suit, holding an attaché case in one hand and a legal binder tucked under his arm was Papademetriou's lawyer. He was a heavyset man with a belly spilling over his belt, an unmemorable face with the exception of thick eyebrows. The female uniformed officer behind the desk, a dark-haired girl in her twenties with a pronounced overbite and prominent cheekbones, looked at the shackled man and the two deputies flanking him with professional disinterest and then returned to her typing.

Captain Jones greeted the two deputies by their first names, and then the lawyer interjected himself between them. "I need to confer with my client in private, gentlemen."

They all followed Captain Jones up the hallway and into a short corridor of pebbled glass doors. He stopped at the last door, opened it, and motioned for the lawyer to go in. The sun was shining through the open blinds of a barred window onto the opposite wall. There was a mahogany conference table in the center of the room with chairs on either side. The lawyer sat down at the table and one of the deputies sat Papademetriou down across from him and then they all left the room.

Captain Jones posted a uniformed officer at the door with instructions to bring Spyridon Papademetriou and his lawyer up to the interrogation room when they were finished. Then he went down the corridor back out into the hallway, walked to the rear of the building, turned a corner, went through a metal door and up a flight of stairs. He opened another door and crossed a hallway to an unmarked door and entered a small, neutrally painted room with no windows. Lieutenant Cransavage and Detective Slivka were waiting for him along with another uniformed officer who was sitting behind a desk in the corner of the room. He folded the newspaper he had been reading, threw it onto the desk, and got to his feet.

"Are we set to go?" Captain Jones asked.

120

"Yes sir," the officer answered and left the room.

In addition to the desk, there was a gun metal gray table with two straight-backed chairs in the center of the room under recessed panels of fluorescent lights, a half dozen more chairs in a row against one wall and a water cooler by the door. On two sides of the table were goose-necked microphones, and in opposite corners of the room where the walls joined the corner of the ceiling, attached to tripod-shaped supports, were video cameras trained on the table.

"Have a seat, boys. He's talking to his lawyer." Captain Jones sat behind the desk and the two detectives sat on two of the chairs against the wall and waited, listening to the hum coming from the air conditioning vents in the ceiling. They didn't have to wait long; ten minutes later, the door opened and the officer brought in Papademetriou, took off his restraints, and told him to take a seat at the table.

"His lawyer wants to be present when he makes his statement," the officer said to Captain Jones.

"That's not necessary," said Papademetriou.

"It would benefit you as well as us to have your lawyer present," Captain Jones said, sitting down across from him.

"I don't need any legal advice...I don't want him interrupting me. I know what I want to say, and I'm going to say it."

"You'll have the opportunity to make a full and complete confession," Captain Jones nodded at the officer. "We all want to wrap this up as quickly as possible. You'll feel better afterwards, and so will we, but we have to follow procedure."

The officer let the lawyer into the room and then was dismissed by Captain Jones. The two detectives picked up their chairs and sat down at opposite ends of the table. Lieutenant Cransavage opened a manila folder and began leafing through papers. The lawyer sat down next to Papademetriou. Captain Jones stood up, went over to the desk where there was a computer terminal and keyboard, hit a key, and then sat down again and pushed a button under the table.

"It's Monday, September fifth," he said into the microphone. "The time is ...2:29 p.m. Present is Spyridon G. Papademetriou, the accused as charged under felony warrants numbers 1023466,

1023467 and 1194456; his attorney, Paul Reutt; Lieutenant Detective John Cransavage, Detective Peter Slivka and Captain Ronald Jones of the Redvale Police Department. Mr. Papademetriou, are you aware these proceedings are being recorded and videotaped?"

"Yes."

"Are all statements you make during these proceedings of your own volition and with benefit of attorney?"

"Yes."

"And are you aware anything you say during these proceedings can be used against you."

"Yes."

"State your address and occupation, Mr. Papademetriou."

"1401 Fourteenth Street, Redvale, Pennsylvania. I was employed at Ross Rosemont and Company until last week; I also worked part-time with the Redvale Phillies."

"In what capacity were you employed with the Phillies?"

"I worked in the cash office."

"Lieutenant..." Captain Jones stood up and switched chairs with Lieutenant Cransavage.

The Lieutenant looked at his paperwork while he spoke. "You participated in the robbery of the Redvale Phillies cash office on the night of August 27th, is that correct?"

"Yes, I did." Could I have some water?"

Captain Jones went over to the water cooler and filled a paper cup and then reached over Papademetriou's shoulder and set the cup on the table.

"And after the commission of the robbery, you then murdered your wife, Sheila; your brother, Stratton; and another man identified as Malcolm Prado."

"Yes, I admit that...." Papademetriou took a sip of water. "But I had nothing to do with Bobby Stuber getting killed or that other man – I want that understood."

"You haven't been charged with those crimes," said Lieutenant Cransavage. "Based on your cooperation –"

"Lieutenant Cransavage," the lawyer leaned in, clearing his throat. "It's been stipulated –"

"Relax, counselor. He hasn't been charged, nor will he be."

"I would like a word with my client."

"I don't want a word with you," said Papademetriou. "I just want it understood, I didn't know anything about it and had nothing to do with Bobby getting killed or that other man getting hurt."

"Understood," Lieutenant Cransavage said curtly. "Now let's go back to the night of August 25th, and I want you to tell us what happened from the beginning to the end to the best of your recollection, and your part in all of it – to the best of your recollection...try to leave nothing out. Detective Slivka or I will only interrupt you if we have a question or need a point clarified."

Papademetriou took another drink of water, wiped his upper lip with his index finger, paused for a deep breath, and started talking. "It was a Thursday – the 25th – I worked in the cash office that night and got home after twelve, so it was actually the 26th – Anyway, Malcolm Prado was waiting for me."

"Had you ever met Malcolm Prado before?" Lieutenant Cransavage asked.

"No," Papademetriou shook his head. "I would've remembered; he had a face you wouldn't forget. He told me when I walked in the door my wife was being held somewhere by his partner – my brother Stratton. He told me if I cooperated in helping them rob the ballpark, my wife wouldn't be harmed; if I didn't cooperate, they'd kill her – they'd kill both of us."

The three police officers looked at one another incredulously. "So they forced you to cooperate by threatening to kill your wife if you didn't help them," Lieutenant Cransavage said in a skeptical tone. "And you believed him about not hurting you or your wife if you cooperated?"

"I had no choice. My wife was my whole life....I had to cooperate even if there was only the slimmest chance he was telling the truth. She was my whole life...." He lowered his head and rubbed the corners of his eyes. The detectives turned their heads almost simultaneously and looked at his lawyer who had a perplexed expression on his face. He was as much in the dark as they were.

"Go on, Mr. Papademetriou," Lieutenant Cransavage prompted him.

"Still...I might've gone to the police anyway," Papademetriou went on. "I can't say for certain I wouldn't have, but then I got a phone call the next morning. Prado was still there. He had spent the night."

"Who called you?" the Lieutenant asked.

"The nurse from our doctor's office asking for my wife," he said, bitterness darkening his face. "It turns out Sheila was pregnant."

"Pregnant?" said the Lieutenant, switching off the microphone "That didn't come up in the autopsy." He switched the microphone back on.

"When I found out she was pregnant everything changed." He was staring past the three men opposite him, focusing on something far removed from the confines of the room. His dark eyes seemed to get darker.

"In what way?"

"I wasn't the father."

Lieutenant Cransavage started to say something, paused, and then asked, "Are you certain of that?"

"I'm sterile," he said flatly. "I believe that's what you call it. I've had all the tests; my sperm count is low." There was an uncomfortable silence in the room, and in that silence you could almost hear the pieces falling into place in the police officers' minds – not all the pieces but most of them.

"Prado left right after the phone call," Papademetriou continued, and all I could think about while I waited for my brother to come by to go over the plan with me was how I'd devoted my life to Sheila, how I'd always tried to give her everything she wanted, how I'd lived for her – She was everything to me, and now I had nothing – It was like my whole life had fallen out from under me." He dropped his eyes to the table and then closed them. He went on speaking in the same toneless voice. "There was only me – me without her, and that wasn't enough, that was nothing, so I decided to kill her because I had nothing left to lose.... I was going to notify the police and let Prado do the job for me, but then I thought, what if he didn't kill her? What if he was bluffing just to get me to cooperate? So I started thinking; I did a lot of thinking while I was waiting for my brother before I finally realized I could start a new life – My old life was over – It didn't exist without Sheila, but I could start a new life. I just needed money; you needed a lot of money to start a new life, and now I knew where to get it."

"So you were an unwilling participant before you found out about your wife," the Lieutenant said. "Then you became a willing participant."

"I came up with my own plan," Papademetriou said coldly. "I just needed to fill in the details, and I was able to do that when my brother came over and gave me the details of their plan. Now all I needed was his help, and I knew I'd get it. He was always one to take the path of least resistance. He was afraid of Prado, afraid Prado was going to double-cross him, but he trusted me – and why not? We were brothers. I'd always been a good brother to him, just like I'd always been a good husband to my wife." He made a face like he'd just swallowed a spoonful of bitter medicine and clenched his fists. "My brother...he loved to get something for nothing. I knew he'd had sex with my wife one second after he came through the door. I could see it in his eyes. He swore up and down that nobody had laid a finger on her, but I knew he was lying. He had the same smirk on his face he always had since we were kids when he thought he was getting away with something. I could've killed him right then, but I needed his help."

"I think you should to stick to the facts as they transpired," the Lieutenant said, "and avoid personal opinion and conjecture."

"I want you to know why I did what I did!" he shouted. "I have to tell it to someone; I have to get it all out."

Mr. Reutt pointed at the Lieutenant. "I think what the detective means is –"

"I know what he means," Papademetriou snapped. "Just let me tell it in my own way...please." Lieutenant Cransavage leaned back in the chair, waiting for Papademetriou to collect himself, and then motioned with his hand for him to continue before folding his arms across his chest. "Their plan was for me to switch places with my brother at the ballpark. First we went through a dry run Friday night. Then Saturday, the 27th, we made the switch in the men's room at the end of the second game while

Malcom Prado hid in one of the supply rooms. Then at a designated time, after my brother got the drop on Bobby – the security guard, and got control of the other employees, he let Prado into the cash room. After they robbed the place, I picked them up outside the park, before switching cars and driving back to the cabin. I knew what Prado was planning once he got back to the cabin. My brother had been very forthcoming when we were alone together – once I'd convinced him I'd take care of Prado. He jumped in with both feet when I told him my plan. I even confided in him about Sheila to make it more convincing. I found it ironic that my brother decided to double-cross Prado because he was afraid Prado was planning to double-cross him only to end up getting double-crossed by me." He looked around the room and smiled weakly. "Don't you find it ironic?" he asked with a trace of anguish in his voice.

"Mr. Papademetriou," his attorney put his hand on his shoulder sympathetically, "why don't you continue?"

"Yes," said the Lieutenant. "Tell us exactly what happened at the cabin on the night of August 27th after the three of you returned from the ballpark with the $185,000 in stolen money."

Papademetriou emptied the cup and then scrunched it in his hand. "Could I have some more water? My throat's a little dry."

Detective Slivka stood up hurriedly and banged his leg on the underside of the metal table. He filled another cup from the water cooler, gave it to Papademetriou, and then sat down rubbing his knee.

"I'll tell you what Malcom Prado thought was going to happen," Papademetriou said, draining the cup of water. "Then I'll tell you what my brother thought was going to happen, and then I'll tell you what actually happened."

"We're only interested in what really happened," said Detective Slivka said.

Papademetriou ignored him. "Prado was planning to kill my wife, then me and probably my brother and take off with all the money. My brother was planning to let Prado take care of my wife, and I would take care of Prado and then cover his tracks for him by confirming to the police what you've already said all the evidence at the crime scene and the cabin pointed to – My wife was abducted and held at the cabin to force me to help Prado and his partner rob the cash office – What else could I do? I had to cooperate if I wanted to see my wife again, and wouldn't any of you have done the same thing? After the robbery, Prado would go back on his word and kill my wife anyway, but after a desperate struggle, I would manage to escape into the woods before his accomplice could shoot me. I'd notify the police when I finally reached a phone, and they'd find my wife's body in the cabin and Prado, too – double-crossed by his partner who'd skipped with all the money. Of course, I'd give the police a phony description of his partner, and meanwhile, my brother could resume his life back in Columbiana and sit on the stolen money until things cooled down, and we could arrange to meet somewhere to split the money."

"We would've asked you to take a polygraph," said Lieutenant Cransavage. "Of course, it's all hypothetical, but do you think we would've believed that story?"

"Maybe...maybe not," Papademetriou shrugged. "But my brother did."

Detective Slivka scratched his head and looked at Lieutenant Cransavage.

"It's hard to keep track of all the double-crossing," Captain Jones said under his breath.

"Mr. Papademetriou," the Lieutenant said in a grave tone. "You murdered three people, including your own brother and wife. Tell us about that."

"There really isn't much to tell," he said, studying the tabletop. "When we switched cars in Redvale after the robbery, Stratton slipped me his gun when Prado wasn't looking. My brother drove us to the cabin in Prado's car. Prado told my brother to keep an eye on me while he went inside. I knew why he'd gone inside, and I knew I'd be next. That was our opportunity, so as soon as Prado went in the door, I gave my brother the beard and he gave me my I.D. tag; we switched jewelry – I became him, and he became me. He thought I was going to march him into the house at gunpoint, get the drop on Prado, and after I shot Prado, he'd take off in Prado's car with the bag of money while I put the place in order, or as much order as I could with

127

two dead bodies in it, and then hide out in the woods before calling the police. He found out I had a different plan when I stuck the gun in his back and marched him into the woods...."

Papademetriou paused, his face relaxing in reflection. He kept his head down, careful to avoid the eyes of the detectives. He sighed deeply and went on, his voice slightly above a whisper. "I can still see that surprised look on his face. It wasn't fear; it was more like shock. He was shocked that I, his brother, was doing this to him. He had that shocked expression on his face right up until I shot him. When Prado heard the shot, he came out and found me on my knees sobbing." He lifted his head and briefly met the gaze of the Lieutenant seated across from him. "The tears were real. I'd just shot Stratton, although Prado thought it was just the opposite. He thought Stratton had shot me when I tried to escape. When he told me Sheila was still alive, I knew I should be the one to shoot her, not Prado. I waited on the porch for him to go into the bathroom, and then I sneaked in behind him. Sheila knew it was me right away. When I pointed the gun at her, she got the same shocked expression on her face as my brother. I pointed the gun at her an extra second before I fired just to let her think about it, let it sink in. I shot her twice – You already know that, and I shot Prado twice. They all had the same surprised looks on their faces – You know...more surprised or shocked than scared."

"What did you do with the weapon?" asked the Lieutenant. "The .38?"

"I threw it in the Schuylkill," he said. "I threw all the guns in the river. Before I did that, I went over the whole cabin to make sure I wasn't leaving any evidence behind. Then I went back into the woods and put my wedding ring and watch on Stratton, the I.D. tag, my shoes – remembering to tie them the right way, and took the fake beard off him. Finally, I wiped my wallet and contents clean of prints, except for that partial print you found, and stuck it back in his back pocket. Before I left, I went over everything in my mind a hundred times to make sure I wasn't overlooking anything. Then I put the money in the trunk of Prado's car and drove all night across state. The next morning, I dumped the contents of the trunk and wiped the car clean of prints and left it in the parking lot of a twenty-four hour supermarket just outside of Pittsburgh and put myself and the bag of money on a bus to Youngstown. From there I took another bus to Columbiana and walked from the bus stop to 221 Sycamore – You were right, of course; Stratton took my place, so it made sense for me to take his place. Monday morning, I called the trucking company where he worked and told them I was quitting. I figured I could live off the money, and if I ever got tired of sitting around, I could find a bookkeeping job somewhere...and that's where you came in."

"Is there anything else you'd like to add?" the Lieutenant asked.

Spyridon Papademetriou slumped back in his chair, his chin on his chest. Fatigue seemed suddenly to be weighing him down. "Just that they deserved to die," he said. "The three of them deserved to die, but I'm sorry about Bobby Stuber and the other man. I never thought anyone else would get hurt."

Captain Jones switched off the mikes and then went over to the desk and hit several keys on the keyboard. After watching him, Detective Slivka turned to Spyridon Papademetriou. "I'm sure their families will be very comforted by your apology."

"Yes," Captain Jones said, shaking his head in disgust. "It's a damn shame the killing wasn't confined to just the people you thought deserved to die." He opened the door and stuck his head into the hallway and a second later an officer came into the room. "Take him down to holding, Murphy." The officer pulled Papademetriou to his feet and started putting the shackles back on him while Captain Jones, Lieutenant Cransavage, Detective Slivka and the attorney huddled together and conferred. As the officer was taking the prisoner from the room, Lieutenant Cransavage called after them, "Just a second."

Spyridon Papademetriou stopped in the open doorway, the officer behind him in the hallway, holding on to his arm. "Do you know why they all had those surprised looks on their faces?" the Lieutenant asked him, not pausing to wait for an answer. "Because you were supposed to be the good guy in this story. They all thought you were the good guy, but in the end it turned out differently. At the end of the story, you turned out to be worse than any of them – That's why." Papademetriou stood slump-shouldered, staring at the floor, not a flicker of emotion on his face until the officer pulled him into the hallway and closed the door behind him. Then he shuffled down the hallway like a weary traveler at the start of a long, hard journey.

The End

CPSIA information can be obtained at www.ICGtesting.com
Printed in the USA
BVOW021457240712

296068BV00001B/6/P